INDECENT PROPOSAL

INDECENT PROPOSAL

AC ARTHUR

www.urbanbooks.net

Urban Books
1199 Straight Path
West Babylon, NY 11704

ISBN-13: 978-1-60162-065-1
ISBN-10: 1-60162-065-9

First Printing August 2008
Printed in the United States of America

10 9 8 7 6 5 4 3 2

Distributed by Kensington Publishing Corp.
Submit Wholesale Orders to:
Kensington Publishing Corp.
C/O Penguin Group (USA) Inc.
Attention: Order Processing
405 Murray Hill Parkway
East Rutherford, NJ 07073-2316
Phone: 1-800-526-0275
Fax: 1-800-227-9604

Acknowledgments

As always I'd like to thank my husband and three wonderful children for their love and continued support. You are my inspiration.

There were so many people who helped me throughout the writing of this story. Eleanor who read the first chapter and told me to go for it. Angelique who is always persuading me not to give up. Gwen who tells me all the time that 'game recognizes game'. This time you were absolutely right! Cheryl for giving the idea two thumbs up. And the readers for their numerous emails that always seem to come at the right time. You are all appreciated.

PROLOGUE

Ladies' Night

"I can't believe it," Cally exclaimed, sinking into the deep cushions of the red couch, that sat against the wall in her cousin's apartment. "Jenna's getting married."

Serena joined her on the other end of the couch, taking a sip from her martini. "Girl, believe it. My invitation came today. What I can't fathom is how last-minute she is. Of course, there was a message on my answering machine from my mother when I came home."

"It's not a big deal," Nola grumbled as she inserted the disk into the DVD player and waited for it to load. "You act like this is the first time somebody in the family is getting married."

"No," Cally interjected. "I think the point is more likely *who* in the family is *not* getting married."

Nola shook her head in agreement and sat in the black leather recliner that was her spot every other Friday night when the cousins met to drink and unwind. "Anyway, I hope this is a good movie this time. You always pick that raunchy stuff, Serena. I keep telling you not everybody has a fetish for groups and bondage like you."

Serena laughed. "You keep saying that, yet you keep showing up to watch whatever raunchy stuff I select." Serena didn't actually consider the movies they watched raunchy. She considered them educational. Especially the ones with the groups. Since her first sexual escapade, Serena had wondered what it would be like to be pleasured by more than one lover, to be touched and kissed and generally fucked senseless in a group. However, she hadn't— even after twenty years of sex—shed all her inhibitions yet.

Nola tossed her an impatient glare. "It's our time together. I'm not about to forego that just because you're a freak."

Cally laughed and almost choked on her glass of Malibu rum and cranberry juice.

"I am not a freak," Serena said with disdain.

"Okay, you're a closet freak," Nola replied.

Cally was waving her hand over her head, trying to get their attention. "Damn, I could die over here and you two would keep right on arguing." She cleared her throat then sat up straight in her chair. "We're all freaks," she announced with a smile. "That's why we gather to watch these movies every other week to learn more tricks for our trade."

All three women laughed at that.

"Who gave her a drink?" Nola said, leaning over to pick up her own glass of wine. "You know she can't hold her liquor."

"I'm not . . . drunk," Cally hiccupped.

"Yeah right," Serena laughed and waited while Nola pressed the play button.

"So Aunt Lorraine called already, huh?"

Serena sighed as she remembered her mother's message. "Yes. And you know what she said so don't even ask."

" 'I sure wish it was my baby getting married,' " Nola mimicked her aunt's high-pitched voice.

"That's exactly what my mother said when she called me this morning," Cally groaned.

"That's what they all say when they get another invitation in the mail. I'm just glad I was in court all day so I didn't have the liberty of hearing my mother's diatribe of why I should be married by now."

Serena spoke up. "Nola, you're always in court or preparing to go to court. That's why you can't have a serious relationship."

Nola glared at Cally then shifted her gaze back to Serena. "First I'm a freak, now I'm a workaholic. You're getting on my nerves tonight."

Serena waved a hand, the rhinestones on her long painted and decorated nails sparkling in the dimly lit room. "You know I speak the truth, that's why you're getting an attitude. You are not going to find love in your office or in that courtroom."

"And you're flitting around town applying makeup to the faces of people you don't know while pining for your ex who left you years ago. So when exactly do you plan on settling down?"

"All right, ladies. The movie's beginning," Cally interrupted.

"Sorry. I forgot this is your only way to release your sexual frustration," Serena said to Cally.

"I like your nerve. I get mine on a regular."

Serena and Nola laughed. "You get yours when you get a chance to look up from that computer. You could probably write a better sex scene then you could act one out." Nola was still laughing as she spoke.

"Shut up! That's not funny," Cally said.

The movie came on and the three women grew quiet

watching the dismal acting skills, impatiently waiting for the action to begin.

For Cally this was a form of release. She was a freelance writer and she barely had time to date, let alone get laid. But when she did she made sure it was enough to last awhile. However, her well was running dry again and she remembered back to her last intimate encounter. It was with Drake, her ex-boss. Drake was good and came running whenever Cally called. With her eyes riveted to the screen, Cally watched as a nicely built ebony-skinned man removed his shirt. Her nipples puckered instantly and she took another sip of her drink. The actor unbuckled his pants and let them fall to the floor. Dude was hung like a horse and Cally's crotch began to pulse. She might be giving Drake a call when she got home tonight.

Serena, on the other hand, thoroughly enjoyed the company of her cousins. They'd grown up together, being the only three girls in the family born within one year of each other. For the most part the Evans family was very close. Jeorge, Randolph, Lorraine, Marsha, Evelyn, and Leola Evans still lived in St. Michael's, Maryland where they were born. Lorraine was Serena's mother, Aunt Marsha was Cally's, and Aunt Evelyn was Nola's. These sisters remained the closest because they had two things in common: They each had one child and that one child was a girl who at beyond thirty years old was still not married.

Normally, Serena tried not to stress over the situation, but now she was dreading Jenna's wedding. Jenna was Aunt Leola's oldest child and she was younger than her, Cally, and Nola by five years, which in Serena's mind meant she was too damn young to be tying herself to one man. But then not everybody had the appetite for variety that she did. Serena prided herself on that variety as she watched the sexy man on-screen. His ass was tight and when he bent over to run his thick tongue between the naked woman's legs she could see his balls stiffen. Serena sighed as her legs began to shake. What she wouldn't do to have her hand wrapped around a sac like that while a man like that ate her pussy.

The every other Friday meeting was just what Nola needed. Her apartment was empty and lonely and she'd much rather sit with her cousins and best friends watching porn than sitting alone in her bedroom masturbating. Since she was sixteen Nola had been able to bring herself to climax. She'd perfected the act to the point that a man was no longer necessary in her life. Her Hitachi Magic Wand, a high-powered vibrator, she'd happily named Bruce, was all she needed. However, she couldn't quite get her mother to understand that, not that she'd tried. She was just getting into the scene on the television as the man inserted his tongue into the woman's center simultaneously slipping a finger into her anus when Serena's voice interrupted.

"We have got to come up with something. There's no way we can show up at that wedding without at least a prospect to get the heat off of us," she said.

"What the hell are you talking about?" Nola asked, irritated that her sexual rush was being interrupted.

"We need to come up with a good reason why we're not married, or . . ." Serena paused ". . . we need to lie and say we're involved with someone so they'll think we're at least close to getting married."

"That's stupid and childish," Nola scolded.

Cally contemplated Serena's words. "But it might work," she added. "I don't know about you but I'd rather not hear my mother's mouth for an entire weekend. Maybe if she thought I was on the right path she'd leave me the hell alone," she said when Nola looked at her questioningly.

"Exactly," Serena said with a satisfied smile in Nola's direction.

"I'm not going to get married to please my mother or yours, for that matter," Nola argued. She wasn't getting married to please anybody. The last thing she wanted was some man dictating to her. She was an independent woman, a defense attorney at the top of her game, no way did she want a man intruding on that.

"We don't have to actually get married. We'll just show up with a guy who will serve as a marriage prospect, so the mothers will get the impression that we are at least trying to find a husband." Serena folded her arms across her chest and sat back trying to keep her mind off the rigorous motion of the actor's ass as he pumped the hell out of the actress. This movie had been on for about twenty minutes now and she had no idea of the sex duo's names. Did one ever know the names of porn actors?

"So all we need is a date for the weekend," Cally offered. "That's not hard."

Nola kept her eyes glued to the screen. The man had pulled out of the woman and was now motioning for her to turn over. Damn, he was certainly hard! He was at least ten inches and thick enough to stretch her fingers were she to grab him. But the woman didn't grab him, instead she grasped the sheets sticking her bottom up further for his perusal. And peruse he did; with his massive hands he spread her cheeks wide. The camera caught a superb angle of her puckered anus and down to her glistening pussy.

Nola swallowed deeply.

The man leaned closer, then stroked her crevice with his tongue. The woman moaned and he repeated the action, this time pausing at her anus, pistoning his tongue inside the tight hole. The woman gritted her teeth and

Nola did the same. In and out his thick tongue swirled inside her, inciting a suckling sound that seemed to echo throughout the room.

Nola sighed, her thighs growing more than moist with the desire that had seeped through her panties. Her own ass tingled as she pictured someone giving her that same treatment. She bit back a moan as she remembered she was not alone.

"Of course we'll have to convince our dates to go along with the pretense of a long-term relationship," Serena added.

"Yeah, that might take a little bribery," Cally said.

Serena smiled and licked her lips. "And not exactly of the monetary persuasion."

Cally smiled too as she read her cousin's thoughts.

"So what do you think, Nola? Are you game?" Cally asked because tonight didn't seem like a good night for Serena and Nola.

Nola rolled her eyes. "Like I said before, I think it's childish and unnecessary. We're adults. We like our lives and there's no reason to be ashamed of that."

Nola was about to move forward with her speech on independence and standing up for themselves when her cell phone rang.

"Nola Brentwood," she answered because she didn't instantly identify the number.

"Hi, Mama," Cally and Serena heard her say.

"I know, Mama, I got my invitation too . . . yes. I'll be there . . . yes. I know Jenna's five years younger than I am." Nola rolled her eyes as she spoke.

Cally and Serena smiled at each other. They didn't need to hear what their Aunt Evelyn was saying. Their mothers had said the same things to them.

Nola disconnected the call and sighed, letting her head

rest on the back of the chair. After a few moments of only the moans coming from the television, Nola finally spoke.

"It'll just be for the weekend and we don't have to sleep with him. We'll just find a date and take him home for the wedding. Then we'll return to our lives just as they are. That's it," Nola said adamantly.

Both Cally and Serena laughed.

"You may not sleep with your date but I figure what's the point in having a man within arm's reach if you can't enjoy him."

The woman on the television moaned just as Serena finished her statement. The man with the big balls stood above her holding his still-swollen dick until come spewed all over the woman's stomach.

Cally sighed. "I definitely agree."

Nola remained silent but felt her own orgasm straining at the surface.

CHAPTER ONE

Just What The Doctor Ordered

It was Monday and Cally had spent most of her weekend thinking of who she could possibly ask to be her date to the wedding. Ladies' night had ended leaving her and her cousins drunk and extremely horny. Even Nola, who had been against having sex with her date, was reconsidering by the time they'd watched both movies.

While Cally claimed to be sexually uninhibited, she had never been a fan of sleeping with strangers. So when trying to come up with a date for the weekend, her mind had instantly had gone to Drake Henderson, who was the senior editor at *Rage* magazine, where Cally had completed a number of assignments over the past year and a half. Their affair—because she refused to think of it as anything more—had begun just one month after they'd first met. The sex came as a result of their second date, when Drake had wined and dined her in historic Federal Hill. It wasn't that Cally was impressed by money, because she made a pretty good living on her own, but Drake was handsome and attentive and had already expressed his willingness to give her any and everything she wanted. That sincere admission and his striking good looks had her itching to share his bed with him that night. And so she did.

Now, months later she was still enjoying their time together, although that time had been drastically cut from the twice-a-week visits to maybe once a month. And Drake wasn't liking that. The last time they were together he'd wasted no time telling Cally how he wanted to take their relationship to another level, for them to get more serious about being together and the possibility of them moving in together. Cally had cringed at his words, then without leaving room for any doubt told Drake that she was not interested in forever.

Why?

She wasn't quite sure, so when he'd asked, she'd begun nibbling on his ear. Knowing that was his spot, it wasn't long before Drake ceased coherent conversation and began the musings of a man about to get his thing off.

Love, marriage, happily-ever-after; none of those were things Cally had given a lot of thought to in her adult life. She'd always wanted to write, so from the third grade until she graduated from college that's all her mind had comprehended. Well, that wasn't entirely all. She'd been introduced to sex early when Thomas Anderson dared her to pull down her shorts in the schoolyard the summer she was in the seventh grade. Cally never shied away from a bet so she'd pulled her pants down and watched in awe as Thomas did the same. They didn't have the same anatomy, of that she was already aware, but Thomas's body sparked a strange heat inside her. So it was no wonder they'd spent the rest of the afternoon behind the building of that schoolyard doing things no twelve-year-old should know.

At any rate, Cally liked her life just fine and hated that

her mother couldn't do the same. Her list of prospects had dwindled as the weekend progressed and then last night, while she'd been editing the article for *Woman's View* magazine, a calendar reminder alerted her to this morning's appointment. And this morning's appointment alerted her to how sexy her gynecologist was.

Cally climbed onto the table and let her legs swing idly at the sides while she waited for Dr. Bradford. The white paper gown crinkled with her movements and she frowned as the starchy material irritated her skin. In just a few minutes her annual GYN exam would be underway. Normally this was not an appointment women would look forward to, but then most women weren't patients of Dr. Steven Bradford.

Her mother would definitely be pleased with him. Hell, Cally would be pleased with him, in her bed at the very least. Steven was tall with a burnt-orange complexion that reminded Cally of the Native Americans pictured on the cover of some of her favorite romance novels. His hair was dark and shaved close to his head. His eyes were a warm brown, his smile downright lethal. And when he talked . . .

Dammit! She was getting wet just thinking about the smooth timbre of his voice.

Jumping down from the table, she hurriedly moved to the paper towel dispenser and was about to wipe away any evidence of her desire when she had a second thought.

If she planned on asking him out for the weekend, why not give him a taste of what he could possibly be getting? Because just like Serena said, there was really no point in having a man to spend the weekend with if you weren't going to get some in the process.

Tossing the unused paper towel into the trash, Cally went back to the table and scooted on top, waiting impatiently for the doctor to arrive.

Before her lascivious thoughts went too far, Cally tried
to concentrate on something else. The very idea of getting off from a GYN exam was a bit disturbing. But knowing that the ever-so-fine Dr. Bradford would soon be
between her legs was wreaking havoc with her common
sense. The crinkly material of the gown rubbed against
her body again, creating an intense friction against her
sensitive skin. Her nipples sprang to life as she squeezed
her legs tightly together in an effort to fight off the increasing pulsating down below.

Dr. Bradford was perfect in all aspects, especially the
one where she needed a date for the wedding this weekend. She wondered how he'd react to her proposal and if
he'd be offended by her request.

"Good morning, Ms. Thomas."

There was that voice. Cally took a steadying breath and
managed a cheerful, if breathy, "Good morning."

Dr. Bradford came into the room with his trusty side-
kick, Ann, trailing dutifully behind him. "If you would lie
back, we can get started," he said, giving her a grim look.

Cally obliged, thinking how much easier this pre-
seduction would be if Ann wasn't in the room. But that
was standard procedure now, to have two medical profes-
sionals in the room with the patient at all times. This was
to cut down on sexual harassment and other indecencies
while the patient was under the doctor's care. For the first
time in her life Cally detested that procedure.

"Slide your bottom down to the edge for me, Ms. Thomas.
Just relax, it'll be over in a few minutes."

His voice floated through the air and Cally almost
sighed. Ann pulled the stirrups from their position on the
side of the table then covered them with socks before
placing Cally's feet inside. Cally appreciated the small
offer of comfort even if she was wishing the woman to dis-

appear. She stared up at the ceiling, trying to think of a way to get Dr. Bradford's attention without Ann noticing. It was her nature to be candid, but in this instance she recognized the need to monitor her words.

"Okay, let your knees fall to the side," Dr. Bradford began. "That's it, just relax. Okay, I'm going to touch you now, let me just warm the speculum."

His voice was as smooth as fine wine, drifting through her body, standing already tense nerves on end. It was as if she recognized his voice intimately. Her breasts felt fuller and heavier, her center throbbed, secreting more of her arousal.

She knew what would happen next and anticipated his touch with bated breath.

The distinctive clinking of metal instruments did nothing to snap her out of her aroused haze. She wanted him to touch her, wanted him to insert the thick metal apparatus into her. She wanted it so badly she almost moaned.

"Okay, I'm going to insert the speculum now. You'll feel a little bit of pressure, that's normal. At any time during the exam let me know if you feel any pain." He peeked above the white gown that covered Cally. "Okay?"

Peering between gapped legs, Cally looked into whiskey-brown eyes. For endless moments they simply stared at each other, then she took a deep breath and dispelled it slowly before whispering, "Okay."

The moment she felt the hard metal against her opening, Cally sighed. Of their own accord her hips lifted slightly and rotated as he slipped the speculum further inside her. Pleasurable sensations soared through her lower region until she was biting on her bottom lip to keep from screaming.

"Okay, we're in. Just relax. Ann, hand me a slide," Dr. Bradford cleared his throat and instructed his assistant.

He sounded different. It was just a faint change in his tone but it was different. Her thighs were gaped open, her arousal clear for him to see; she felt sexier now than she ever had in her life. Something about the way he had an unfettered view of her, how he was in complete control of the most intimate region and yet they were forced to do everything but enjoy it.

He removed the speculum slowly, torturously. Cally kept her eyes closed, her tongue stroking over her bottom lip the way she wanted his to stroke her. She heard the speculum fall into the bowl Ann held and could picture the woman turning away from the table where she lay to place the bowl near the door.

It was in that instant that she felt it.

The lightest touch against her clit.

Her eyes shot open and she peered once again between her legs. Smoldering brown eyes met her gaze and held it as his finger again—this time boldly, purposefully—stroked the tightened bud.

Cally shivered then rotated her hips again and watched as his eyes darkened.

So much for the myth that a GYN exam was simply another form of torture for a woman. Dr. Bradford had just unknowingly spoiled Cally for any other doctor's visit for the rest of her life. She hadn't questioned he was the right man to ask for her weekend away and now she knew it with even more certainty. It would take, at the very least, the entire weekend for her to have Dr. Bradford the way she wanted him.

The sound of Ann's movements interrupted them and Dr. Bradford pulled his hand away, holding those same fingers that had just stroked her out to Ann for distribution of the gel.

Cally bit her bottom lip, knowing full well that Dr. Bradford was aware of just how lubricated she already was down there. Still, she continued to anticipate his next touch.

"I'll be using my fingers for the next part of the exam. Let me know how it feels . . . I mean, if you feel any pain." Just above the starchy white covering Dr. Bradford's eyes met hers again.

Her palms flattened on her stomach as she closed her eyes waiting, wanting, needing . . .

Inserting his fingers inside of her, he pressed gently on her stomach. *Oh God*, Cally thought, she was going to lose herself right this very moment. *Please, don't stop,* she prayed while working her PC muscles against his finger.

This time he pulled out of her abruptly and before her eyes could open all the way he was standing closer, inserting those same two fingers into her rectum. Cally's mind reverted back to the actress in one of the porn movies they'd watched on Friday, when the man had finger-fucked her in both her holes simultaneously. Cally had become so aroused she almost stripped her clothes off and masturbated in Serena's living room. The actress looked like she was enjoying one hell of an orgasm as the actor had pumped his fingers inside of her. And when she came her essence had oozed down her thighs until the actor had bent over and licked it up. Cally's thighs shook, her stomach quivering as she strained not to explode on the examining table.

Dr. Bradford apparently knew how close she was as well. He removed his fingers, staring at her with a conspiratorial glare. He looked as if he wanted to smile, as if he had received just as much satisfaction from the supposed exam as she had. She opened her mouth to ask him that very question when she heard Ann's voice from beside her.

"Put your legs down and lift your right arm."

Cally had almost forgotten the woman was in the room with them but quickly did as she was told.

He was removing his gloves now and came to stand on her right side. "I'm going to do your breast exam next," he said cordially.

But in her mind the words translated to, "*Let me fondle your breasts.*"

"Sure," was her breathy reply.

His fingers moved methodically in circular motions around the base of her right breast and toward her nipple. Cally watched him. His expression was tight, devoid of any apparent emotion; still he kept his eyes trained on hers. Thick eyelashes shadowed warm brown eyes, thin-rimmed glasses sat atop a straight aristocratic nose and his perfectly shaped goatee surrounded full lips. Her mouth watered.

"Okay, you're all done. Get dressed and I'll be back in to talk to you."

And just like that he was done. Cally remained on the examining table a few minutes after she'd been left alone and tried to pull herself together. Her center still pulsed and her breasts tingled where his hands had so intimately touched just moments before.

Taking a deep breath, she raised herself up from the table and on wobbly legs started to slip on her underwear. Then she thought about the look he'd given her before he left the room. Something had definitely changed between her and the good doctor, something that would ultimately work to her advantage. She pulled her dress over her head and hastily stuffed her panties into her purse.

In his office down the hall, Steven Bradford sat behind his desk trying desperately to concentrate. He was supposed to be a professional—had taken the Hippocratic oath swearing to be such. He was not supposed to be attracted to her. He was her doctor and nothing more.

Yeah right. Tell that to the mammoth erection currently pressed painfully against his zipper. Gripping the bulge, he shifted until he could breathe a little easier. She trusted him to render his medical opinion where she was concerned. She did not expect him to think about sinking his length into her hot pussy. Then again, he wasn't expecting her to be so wet, so openly available to him. From the moment he'd looked between her legs he'd known something was different. Her nether lips were swollen with arousal, kissable, her hole oozing with desire. All of which led him to wonder what she'd been thinking before he came in.

Steven dragged a hand over his face, trying to get a grip. He was a gynecologist and a man, so he knew the signs of a woman aroused very well. Her legs had been opened wide as if she were waiting specifically for him. Her labia glistened, exuding an intoxicating scent that pulled him closer. For one extremely prolonged moment he'd been tempted to bend his head and taste her.

Luckily, Ann was at his side, her presence reminding him of his duties. He performed the examination even though his mind was so beyond anything medical it was insane. Just one touch, one silent question and he'd received his answer. Her clitoris had been tight, plump and delectable and when he'd grazed it all blood ceased flowing through his body, pooling at his groin, demanding attention. She hadn't yelled harassment and she hadn't punched him, all signs that said she was thinking along the same lines he was.

His heart beat erratically at that thought.

For the last two years Calathia Thomas had been his patient. He knew everything there was to know about her, including the fact that she was beautiful and desirable and hot as all the hookers on Baltimore's famous block.

Steven tried to shake free of those thoughts as he stood and prepared to go talk to her. He was rock-hard and aching to find release. He was also fairly certain that something highly unethical was about to happen between him and Ms. Thomas. What really surprised him was the fact that he didn't care to stop it. Steven was a man sure of his prowess with women. He enjoyed sex and enjoyed really hot, kinky sex even more. But he wasn't the type of man to take such an intimate act lightly, so thoughts of fucking his sexy patient had him more than a little confused.

As he walked down the hall, Steven tried to find some sort of excuse for this attraction, some reason he could give for these traitorous sensations he was feeling. Letting himself into the room, he pulled the chair a good two feet away from her and sat down with her chart in his lap. "Well, Ms. Thomas, it appears you're in tip-top shape. We'll have the blood work back tomorrow and I'll call you if there are any problems." He looked at her to see if everything he'd thought had happened earlier had been his imagination.

Her eyes masked nothing as she openly perused him. She smiled when she noticed him staring and then let her gaze drop to the bulging erection he did not attempt to hide. She was bold and candid . . . traits he appreciated in a woman.

"Is there a problem, Ms. Thomas?" he asked.

Cally slipped off the chair, walking toward him with slow, purposeful steps. He was hard and ready and she was wet and impatient. All he had to do was say the word and she'd straddle his lap and ride him into oblivion. She took a deep breath, trying to get her priorities in order, then paused and leaned over so that her face was just a breath away from his.

"I actually do have a problem, Dr. Bradford."

Steven removed his glasses and slipped them into his jacket pocket. He sat back in the chair and glared at her. She smelled sweet and enticing. He put her medical chart on the table beside him and let his hands fall to his thighs. "And what exactly is your problem?"

Cally smiled and wet her lips. She lifted the hem of her dress until it rode around her hips, displaying her panty-free center. His eyes didn't leave her face and she felt her wetness oozing down her thighs. He wasn't overly anxious, which told her he was no stranger to women offering themselves to him. That thought bothered her for a split second, then she shrugged it off and straddled him. "I need a date for the weekend."

"You of all people should not have a problem getting a date." His hands fell to her thighs, his thumbs skimming the soft inside skin. "Tell me what you really want," he said, lowering his voice.

Hot for him did not begin to describe what Cally was feeling, but all this talking was killing her buzz. "How about I just show you," she suggested, then proceeded to unzip his pants.

His dick sprang free and rested heavily in her hands. He creamed at the tip and she wanted to dip her head to take the white drop into her mouth. Instead she rubbed her finger over it then slipped that same finger into her mouth. She was stroking his length and enjoying the taste of him on her tongue when he slipped two fingers inside her moistened center.

"I think I'd rather be the one doing the showing," he said, then bent forward and bit her distended nipple through her blouse.

That was it, Cally wasn't waiting another moment. To hell with the fact that he was her doctor and the fact that they were in the examining room and the door wasn't locked . . . that thought actually aroused her even more. "Foreplay will have to wait, Dr. Bradford. I want you now."

Steven only smiled at her, a patient, alluring smile that pricked her heart. "I don't like rushing, Ms. Thomas." He lifted her off his lap and placed her on the table, being careful to keep her skirt yanked above her hips. Taking measured steps across the room, he locked the door and returned to her.

"I especially want to take my time figuring out why you need a date." He pulled the stirrups out of their holding while he spoke, then slowly placed each one of her feet. With his hands on her knees, he pushed her thighs open. He looked down at her center and she saw his jaw clench.

"Beautiful," he whispered. "You are very wet, Ms. Thomas. Is that all for me?"

Cally inhaled deeply. He wasn't even touching her, yet she was aroused beyond measure. "If you want it," she said with a shaky breath.

"No," he said adamantly, then shifted his gaze from between her legs to her face. "Tell me if it is for me."

That smooth voice Cally had adored changed, deepening into a commanding pitch that made her nipples hard. "It's for you," she conceded without hesitation.

He kept his gaze level and said, "Give it to me."

For a moment she was confused. Here she was legs up in the air, her pussy bared for him and anyone else with a key to that door to see, what else did he want?

His brown eyes darkened and one brow raised. She nodded with realization and lay back on the examining table, scooting her bottom close to the edge just like she had earlier during the exam. Her legs were spread wide, giving him a view he'd seen before. He probably wanted more, she knew she did. So moving her hands down she touched her nether lips, spreading them open for him.

She didn't have a moment to ask if she'd done what he wanted, because in the next second his mouth was on her, his tongue slurping up her arousal in slow, lingering strokes. Cally moaned and lifted her hips slightly.

"Don't move," he commanded and pulled back. "You said this was for me, let me take it the way I want."

Damn! Cally's breasts heaved, her hands instinctively going to the turgid nipples to squeeze. She was not one for letting a man talk to her any kind of way, but she was definitely feeling Dr. Bradford's assertiveness. She immediately stilled her movements, resigned to let him take what he wanted, how he wanted.

With deft precision his fingers slipped inside her. No longer was it the professional touch of her doctor, now there was only the heat. The scorching trail his touch, his tongue, left on her. She bit her lip to keep from screaming as he pressed deeper and deeper inside.

She wanted to move against his hand, to speed up the motion and come all over him, but his previous words kept her still. She was on fire, raging against a war of desire she'd never experienced before. And she loved it.

Steven pulled his fingers out of her with a distinct plop, then lowered his head again, putting his warm mouth to her scorching crotch. His hands gripped her thighs, pushing them further apart. His tongue drove deep, filling her similarly to the way his finger just had. She gasped and this time couldn't resist moving her hips against the orchestration of his mouth.

It was torture, his tongue inside her hole, his hands moving to grasp her butt, lifting her as if she were the most succulent entrée on the buffet bar. He tilted his head as his mouth made love to her pussy. She was drenched with desire and he lapped it up greedily. She heard herself moaning just seconds before he caught her clit between his lips and sucked.

The moans grew louder regardless of the fact that she was in a doctor's office and there were people in the waiting room as well as Steven's assistant, who might have been just beyond that door. None of that mattered, all she could focus on now was how fantastic it was going to feel when she came. And with the tumultuous building of lust he orchestrated that would surely be any minute now.

CHAPTER TWO

Teaching Serena

So Serena didn't have a date in mind when she'd proposed this scheme to get over on her relatives. How difficult could it be to find a man willing to spend the weekend with her? She wasn't bad-looking, in fact, she'd say she was downright fine! With her salon-dyed auburn hair that rested on her shoulders in soft curls and her light-brown eyes and chocolate-toned skin, she knew she was straight in the looks department. She worked out religiously so her size-eight body was plump in all the right places and tight in the others.

No, she did not anticipate a problem at all.

"Hey, Rena, long time no hear from."

His voice rubbed her skin as if he were right there beside her. James Baker, her high school sweetheart, could turn her on even when he was hundreds of miles away.

"I just moved back to town and was wondering if we could hook up. Give me a call when you get the message. I'm looking forward to reminiscing about old times."

Serena sat on her bed with a definite plop. James was back in B-more, she couldn't believe it. What had it been, six, no seven, years since she'd last seen him? His voice, still echoing in her ears long after the answering machine had clicked off. The first thing she remembered was that devilish cleft in his chin. He loved it when she ran her tongue over that spot while simultaneously rubbing his balls. He was tall, just like she liked her men, with skin like shining onyx. His body was built extremely well for a teenager. She could just imagine what it looked like now.

Wasn't it funny that James would call her this week, when she was in desperate need of a date? Her mother had always liked James. Actually, what she really liked was the way he sang with the church choir. James did have a nice voice to go along with that nice body and those oh-so satisfying moves in bed.

He'd been Serena's first and by far the best. Never in a million years would she forget the things James had introduced her to or the one thing she'd staunchly refused. Years and several lovers later Serena still wasn't ready to even consider the possibility. But that was neither here nor there. She needed a date and James was just as good as the next guy, if not better.

As she dialed the number he'd left she wondered what had made him come home. Maybe his music career had crashed and burned. And he was now penniless and desperate. Maybe he saw this date thing as a way to extort money from her. Under no circumstances would she pay for a date with cash, that seemed too much like prostitution.

But the thought quickly fled her mind. James was a very talented singer and songwriter. She didn't readily believe that he hadn't had any success in the years he was away. Still, she considered the possibility that he would want some type of payment for his services. If that payment was in the form of sex, she was definitely game. Now while it probably should have, that did not constitute prostitution in her wicked little mind. Sex with James had always been mutually satisfying, which would make this arrangement more like a professional exchange.

Serena hummed as the phone continued to ring. It was a tune that she and James had loved when they were a couple. She tried not to make much of the fact that she hadn't thought about that song in years and was now humming it as if she'd just heard it.

James answered on the third ring.

"Hello, stranger," she said cheerfully.

"Rena! Damn, it's good to hear your voice, baby girl."

James always called her *baby girl* and she always blushed when he did. "You would have heard my voice more often if you'd called more."

"I know. I know. Don't start nagging me, my mother is doing enough of that. So how've you been?"

"I've been good. How about you? What brings you back home?" There was no use beating around the bush. Serena realized she needed to know his financial and personal situation right off the bat. The last thing she wanted was drama over calling some female's man.

"I'm cool. I just missed the city. L.A. really isn't my style."

"It took you seven years to figure that out. And where's your woman? Did you leave her in L.A. and does she know you're calling me?"

"Hold on a minute." James chuckled. "You sound like a reporter."

Serena shrugged. "Sorry. I just wanted to get all the preliminaries out of the way."

"I hear you. I don't have a woman, not in L.A. and not

here. It took me seven years to figure out my place in the music industry was not as a singer. I like writing better and I can do that from any location. Now your turn, where's your man 'cause I know you've got one."

She smiled. "If you know I've got one then why did you call me?"

"Because a part of you will always belong to me, no matter who the flavor of the month happens to be. So like I said, where is he?"

A part of you will always belong to me. Why did his possessiveness still sound so sweet? "Well, you're wrong. I don't have a man. But I do need one for the weekend."

James laughed. "You need one for the weekend? What's that about?"

"My cousin's getting married and I don't want to go back to St. Michael's alone."

"Your cousin? Which one? I know that mean-ass Nola hasn't found a husband before you?"

It was Serena's turn to laugh. Nola and James had a hate-hate relationship that went way back to elementary school. "No, Nola's not getting married. It's Jenna. You know, my Aunt Leola's daughter."

"Oh, yeah, I remember her. She's younger than us, right?"

Serena groaned. "Don't remind me."

"So why do you need somebody to go home with you? Your family is cool and they cook up a storm when something like this goes down."

"I know. But Mama's been on me about settling down and I don't feel like hearing the speech this weekend. So will you go with me?"

James was silent for a minute. "You aren't getting any younger, Rena. Maybe you should be thinking about finding the right guy and starting a family."

Serena pulled the phone away from her ear and stared

at it a moment. Then she shook her head because he wasn't there to see the crazy look she was giving him. "Please, you are the last person to talk about settling down when you've been jetting across the country for years. I just need you to go back to St. Michael's with me for the weekend and act like we've been seeing each other again."

"I'd like for us to be seeing each other again."

Serena paused. Something in James's voice was different. He was usually carefree and unrestrained. Now he sounded serious and contemplative. She couldn't tell right off if she liked that or not.

"We can," she said instantly, "this weekend, I mean."

James was quiet for a minute. "I'll do it, if you'll do something for me."

Serena felt an instant of dread then pushed it aside; surely he'd grown past that or at the very least experienced it with someone else by now. "What do you want?"

"I want you to spend the night with me. Tonight. At my place."

She was silent.

"Spend the night with you doing what?" she asked cautiously.

"Come on, Rena. You know how we used to kick it. Didn't I say in my message that I was looking forward to reminiscing with you?"

A small smile touched her lips as she admitted she was looking forward to that too and that was the real reason why she'd called him back so quickly. "If I had a man you wouldn't be able to reminisce with me."

"Girl, please, no man will ever do you like I do."

"You're still cocky," she giggled.

"And you still like it."

More than he knew, she sighed. "Okay, give me the address, I'll be there."

* * *

Three hours later Serena raised her hand to knock on James's door. She had no doubts or misgivings about what she was about to do. She would sleep with James tonight and through the weekend if she had to and not just because she needed a date. While she'd showered and dressed she realized she still needed this. She needed James.

At least she needed sex with James. That's all she would concede to.

They'd been young and what they called "in love" once. He'd been her first and had taught her more than any other man she'd ever been with since. For that alone he would always hold a very special place in her heart. But that was it. She was not hung up on him. If she was, she would have been crushed when he announced he was going to California and hadn't even offered to take her with him.

If she were still hung up on James she wouldn't be able to sleep with other men the way she had in the years he'd been gone—even if they never made her feel the way he did.

If she were still hung up on James she would be breaking her neck to see him as soon as she possibly could. Wait a minute, she thought as she knocked, then quickly pulled her hand back, wasn't she doing exactly that?

"Hey, baby girl," he said with a sexy grin as he opened the door.

Serena cleared her throat and took a deep breath. He looked even better than she remembered. "Hello."

James frowned as if he was offended. "Is that all the greeting I get?"

Serena willed herself to relax. It was just James and this was just going to be sex. "Damn, I just got here," she sighed as James pulled her into his embrace.

It was just James, just his strong arms carefully enfolding her, his purely masculine scent sifting through her nostrils, increasing the potency of the memories they shared. It wasn't anything fabulous. It wasn't the reunion of a great love affair. And it definitely wasn't their destiny. Her insides quivered as her nipples became sensitive brushing against his chest, thus verifying that it was just sex.

Then his mouth claimed hers, his tongue tracing a sleek line over her bottom lip, then tugging at it while he growled. Her mind whirled with more thoughts of how this was just sex and nothing else while her body seconded that. Her hands came up around his neck, pulling him closer, almost begging for more.

With luscious strokes his tongue traced her teeth, her upper lip, and her bottom one again. She sighed with contentment and opened her mouth to him. Their tongues met in a fiery duel, twisting and twining until moaning filled the room. Rena couldn't tell hers from his, nor did she bother to figure it out.

Kissing James had always been like a slice of heaven. In all her years of sexual encounters she'd never been kissed into an orgasm, like she had with James. Was it the thickness of his lips? Or the smooth seductiveness of his tongue? The tilt of his head, the touch of his hands? She had no clue but at this very moment her panties were drenched with arousal, her pussy pulsating with expectation.

She was about to grind her aching center against him when he abandoned her mouth, tracing a firey path along her jaw.

"It's good to see you, Rena," he whispered into her ear, his hands caressing her back.

Her fingers tightened in the material of his shirt. She

inhaled his scent again and was grateful that he was holding her so tightly, otherwise her now weak knees would
have forced her to the floor. "It's good to see you too," she
admitted.

"Come on in and get comfortable," he said, releasing
her and closing the door as she made her way into the living room.

His apartment was still pretty much empty and she
dropped her bag near the one table in the huge space she
presumed was his dining room. Taking a few more steps,
she figured she was in the living room since there was a
couch and a fifty-two-inch flat-screen television. "I hope
you plan on furniture shopping soon."

He stood near the table and Serena almost sighed again
when she spotted him there. One hand was thrust into the
pocket of his jeans—jeans that wore him instead of the
other way around—his muscled thighs and long limbs
filled out the denim material like Serena was sure no other
man could. He wore a simple polo shirt but the muted
butter color seemed to enhance his dark tone, lending a
soft yet masculine air to him.

He assessed her in much the same way as she was doing
him. She'd changed from her slacks and blouse that she'd
worn to work and now wore a silk shirt dress and sandals.
The soft material brushed against her skin and she wished
it were his hands. His glare devoured her as if feeding off
the simple sight of her. That made her center pulse and
her legs tremble—the thought of James feeding off her
was too arousing for words.

With James she had always experienced an overindul-
gence of sexuality. Once upon a time that had scared her
to death because only James could make her consider
doing outrageous things. However, in the past years she'd
experimented some and indulged in movies for the stuff

she still hadn't gotten the nerve to try. Some of those things she'd imagined doing one day, but was perplexed by the fact that the only person she imagined doing them with was James.

But she didn't want to think about that now. "Are you going to answer me?" she said when they'd stood staring at each other for way too long.

"Huh?" he said quizzically.

"I asked you if you were going to buy some furniture anytime soon."

"Nah." He shook his head and moved closer to her. "I really haven't been thinking about furniture."

"What have you been thinking about?" she asked when he was only a breath away from her.

"You," he said simply and toyed with a heavy curl that rested near her ear. "Us."

"There is no more us," Serena informed him, wondering if that was what he wanted to hear.

"But there was," he said, his voice lowering until it was a mere whisper over her skin. "Don't you remember what we were like together?"

She remembered all too well. "We were young."

"And?"

"And we didn't know what we wanted or needed." *Or how badly it would hurt if we didn't get it.*

"I knew then that I wanted you." He leaned forward and kissed her cheek, then let his tongue lead a heated path to her ear. "I know now that I want you."

Serena sighed. There was no denying the chemistry between them was still there and she had no intention of doing so. He said he wanted her. She wanted him. There was no disagreement there.

She lifted her hands to his shoulders and squeezed. "We never had a problem in this department, did we?"

His tongue was creating sinful swirls of warmth down her neck as his hands spanned her waist. "I don't recall us having any problems."

Serena gave a shaky laugh. "You always were delusional." Her eyes closed to the pleasure of his tongue on her skin.

"You used to say I was imaginative. Now you've moved on to something else."

"You are many things, James Baker." He cupped her bottom and she moaned. "Most of them are indescribable."

He chuckled. "I like being imaginative better."

"Really?"

James murmured something into her hair as his fingers deftly lifted the hem of her skirt until she felt coolness against her bottom. "Nice," he said, looking down at her plump cheeks bared by the black thong she wore.

Serena had a quiet sex appeal that had a way of creeping up on him and choking him all at the same time. He'd known she was a virgin when he'd first approached her in the eleventh grade and when he'd kissed her he'd known he would be the one to break her in, he had to be.

Teaching Serena Clark the joys of sex became a daily task for him, one he gladly indulged in before any schoolwork. She was passionate and willing and eager and desirable, she was everything. And he'd walked away from her. Never would he understand the foolishness of his youth.

But that was done. He was back and she was here with him. He'd been thinking about Serena Clark for months now and if this was the only way he could get back into her life he was willing to go for it.

James recalled how much he'd taught Serena in their time together. He also recalled the one lesson she'd been too shy to participate in. She'd always refused when he brought it up. James originally thought she was afraid but then he knew her too well for that. She wasn't afraid, she just wasn't sure. Of him, of herself, of what they had together. Tonight he was going to change all of that.

"I have something for you," he whispered, then tore his gaze away from her gorgeous behind.

"What?" She looked up at him with aroused eyes and he simmered.

He couldn't wait to be inside of her again, couldn't wait to feel her legs wrapped around his waist, her walls tightening around his dick. But he would wait. This lesson he had for her—for both of them—was important enough for that.

Serena was prepared for sex. She was even prepared for the emotional toll sex with James would obviously take on her. They had a history, one that she could not deny. She'd dreamed of the day when he came back to Baltimore because she'd known that he would, eventually.

When he left they hadn't said they would keep in touch, so the fact that he hadn't written and barely called her wasn't as much of a betrayal as it could have been. She still didn't understand why he'd never asked her to come along or why they didn't try to have a long-distance relationship, even if it probably wouldn't have worked. But none of that mattered now.

All she needed now was a date for the weekend and this was James's way of getting payment for that act. So be it, she wouldn't make this temporary connection between them any bigger than it needed to be. She couldn't afford to.

He kissed her then. A brush of lips that instantly turned into a heated battle between tongues and teeth. Serena slanted her head, taking his tongue deeper into her mouth.

He sucked her lips, first the bottom, then the top before wrapping his lips around her tongue and sucking until her head swooned from the delicious sensations.

When he pulled away from her she clung to him to keep from slipping to the floor.

"Come with me, baby girl." He led her to the shower where he set the water, then undressed her and put her inside.

She didn't need another shower but Serena moaned as the warm water hit her sensitive skin. James seemed to be different than when they were together before. He was definitely more attentive, although he'd always been aware of her needs. Now it seemed magnified in the way he took his time undressing her and gently lifting her into the shower. She attributed that to the fact that they'd both matured and that providing Cokes and snacks during their marathon sex sessions wasn't impressive anymore.

Tonight he lifted her out of the shower, drying her off with a huge, fluffy white towel before leading her back to the bedroom where only a four-poster bed stood in the middle of the floor. She'd commented on his lack of furniture again to which she'd received a cocky grin and this flippant remark, "The most important piece of furniture is right here."

He'd positioned her on the bed, which Serena had to admit was grand and beautiful, with its heavy cherrywood moldings and soft chocolate-brown comforter. There were plenty of pillows, all in different hues of brown, all soft and inviting as James pushed her naked body down upon them. He hovered above her and her breath caught at what she thought she saw in his eyes.

"I really did miss you, Rena," he said in a voice that was too gravelly and too emotional for her comfort.

"Well, you're home now." She tried to sound casual but the swelling of her heart made it impossible.

"That's right. I'm home."

He brushed his lips gently over hers.

She trembled and her eyes fluttered shut. Before she had the chance to open them again James had shifted and then she felt something cool and soft against her cheek. Her eyes opened just in time to see darkness engulf her as he slipped a silk sash around her head and tied.

Serena's heart beat rapidly. She'd never been blind-folded before.

"What are you doing?" she asked.

"You still trust me, don't you?"

Serena hesitated. She hadn't seen James in years but deep down she knew he was the same boy she'd gone to the high school football games to watch play. "Yes, I trust you."

"Then lay back and enjoy. I have something very special for you tonight."

Because her body was now humming with a sexual energy she'd never before experienced, Serena did just as she was told. Laying her head back against the soft pillow, loving the feel of the plush comforter beneath her, she whimpered when his hands grasped her right wrist. Again she felt the cool slickness of silk as her hand was tied to the bedpost. He repeated this action with her other hand. She couldn't see him and now she couldn't touch him, either. Serena was beyond turned on, her mind racing with scenarios, her body anticipating the possibilities.

Nola's words about her secretly liking bondage echoed in her head. She had watched many movies where the actress was tied up or enslaved in some manner while the actor did as he pleased with her. From light spankings to whips that encouraged submission, Serena found herself entranced by the extreme arousal the actress, and she herself, received.

"Tonight I want you to focus only on what you feel," James whispered, indulging in the sight of her exposed body.

His Rena had definitely changed with time. She always had a nice body, but now it was more mature, sexually ripe. Her legs had spread without his command, her bottom creating an enticing curve that spanned out to her thick thighs. He remembered those thighs, remembered their softness and couldn't wait to feel them against his cheeks again.

"I don't want you to think about the wedding, this weekend or even tomorrow. Just concentrate on here and now." James inhaled a shaky breath as he studied her heavy breasts, the huge dark-brown circles in their center and the thick long nipples. He swallowed and fought like hell to keep from taking the erect skin into his mouth. She shifted her legs again, spreading them even wider and his heart did a triple flop in his chest. Her pussy was neatly shaved so that only a shadow of hair was left lingering into the valley between her legs. She opened like a just-blossomed flower, sweet nectar glistening against her petals.

His jaw clenched as he again resisted the urge to touch, to taste, just one time. Instead he slipped off the bed and moved to the door.

Serena heard the quiet and knew she was in the room alone. She should probably call him but she was fairly sure he hadn't left her there as some sort of cruel joke. *Cruel* being the operative word, since her pussy throbbed with wanting and her nipples ached with need. If her hands weren't tied she'd touch herself to afford some sort of relief to this burning deep inside that had begun with his phone call.

Shifting to the side she let one heavy breast rub against the comforter, enjoying the light friction against her very aroused skin. Heat continued to pool in her center so she clamped her legs closed tightly then needed desperately to feel something entering her, so she opened her legs and let the air cover the accumulating moisture. The contrast between hot and cool had her out of control and she undulated her hips as if James were deep inside her.

She heard movement in the room again and stilled.

"James," she whispered.

"I'm right here, baby girl."

He sounded like he was across the room and she struggled to lift herself only to feel pressure on her shoulders, pushing her back down onto the bed. The pressure wasn't hard or overwhelming but it was pointed and left no room for argument. Not that she was planning on arguing because after being pushed into the pillows she felt a finger stroke her clit and all sane thought fled from her mind.

"Yes," she breathed and opened her legs wider. "Touch me there."

The finger moved slowly up and down, touching the tip of her tightened bud then sliding sinuously down to her moist opening. It didn't dip inside, although Serena was sure she'd requested it to. Instead it grazed her anus then came back up to her clit to start all over again.

Her head flung from side to side as she anxiously waited for him to either replace that finger with his tongue or his dick. She remembered how big James was. How thick and long he grew, especially when she licked on his ear. That memory had her center creaming and she heard him moan. Then she felt the pointed tip of a tongue brushing against her clit and down toward her opening. Serena sighed audibly as her arousal was lapped up diligently. She bit her bottom lip and moaned because she couldn't grab his head and hold him to the spot that afforded her so much pleasure.

That skillful tongue began to swirl, covering every moistened crevice of her juncture. Serena lifted her hips to meet the motion of the tongue. Following her lead, the tongue slipped deep inside of her and Serena's entire body began to shake. Her feet were planted firmly on the bed, her lips slightly lifted as that tongue plunged in and out of her like a piston.

Her moans became screams, her head thrashing wildly on the pillows. "James! Please! Now!"

"Focus, baby," she heard him whisper. "Just focus on how good it feels."

Serena was focusing. She was focusing on the intense sensations soaring through her body. She was focusing on the warm heat his tongue provided and on how badly she wanted his thick dick inside her. She was . . . wait a minute . . .

"James?" she called to him again.

"Yes, baby girl. I can see you're enjoying it. Tell me how it feels."

While having her pussy eaten—correction, being feasted on in grand style—was something Serena thoroughly enjoyed, her thoughts had shifted slightly. James sounded aroused, he sounded as turned on as she felt, he sounded . . . a distance away.

"It feels real good," she offered, wanting to hear him speak again.

"Yeah? You look good spread out like that. You look real good."

There was no way in hell James could speak that clearly

with his tongue buried inside her. She shifted again because that tongue grazed the walls of her vagina just right.

"Do I really look good, baby?" she asked coyly.

James groaned. "Oh, yeah. You look good."

Serena moaned. She was momentarily filled with uncertainty while at the same time sure she'd never been this aroused before in her life. "How do I taste, James?"

"Mmmm."

She heard the moan and stilled. That didn't sound like James.

She was about to rattle off the first of a million questions when she felt the cool silk slipping from her eyes. She blinked and focused saw James hovering above her face. He leaned over and kissed her, thrusting his tongue deeply into her mouth just as another tongue thrust deeply into her core.

Her eyes widened and she noticed him watching her even as he attempted to kiss her senseless. At that moment her legs were spread even wider, a thumb fiercely rubbed her clit and that masterful tongue stroked her labia, her core, her very essence.

Serena's body was on fire, her mind rapidly trying to decipher what was going on. James was kissing her, he was squeezing her breasts, pinching her nipples. But then someone else was licking her crotch—actually, they were draining her completely but that was getting a little too technical.

"James," she murmured against his lips.

"It feels good, doesn't it, baby girl?"

Serena couldn't answer because his tongue was again mating seductively with hers.

She was breathless when he pulled back and stared at her with passion-filled eyes. "Did Sherry make you feel good?"

His words stunned her and for a minute she wanted to cuss him out. The one thing she and James had adamantly disagreed on was bringing a third party into their intimate relationship. She'd never given him a reason, simply refused to even consider it. And now . . .

Fingers, she had no idea how many, thrust inside her and she screamed, then panted as her release came in thick soul-shattering waves. Amazed by what had just happened, but too pleased to complain, Serena moaned, "She made me feel damned good!"

And Rena's words made him feel the same. When James had decided to come back to Baltimore he'd thought of nothing else but getting back with Rena. He remembered their lovemaking as if it were only yesterday, when they both began exploring the wonders of sex.

He had always been more adventurous than Rena and wanted desperately to share all his sexual exploits with her. So he'd promised himself that if he and Rena got the chance to be together again he would make his preferences known right off the bat.

Sure it was a gamble, bringing another woman into their bed so soon, but James figured it was a gamble that would pay off in the long run. Yes, he loved Rena, more than life itself and if she'd said she wasn't down for the threesome he would have backed off, keeping his fetish to himself as best he could.

Lucky for him, Rena was as passionate and adventurous as he'd known she could be.

CHAPTER THREE

Conference Call

For about the millionth time today Nola thought back to the three-way telephone conversation she, Cally, and Serena had last night. Besides the fact that her hornier-than-hell cousins were one step ahead of her—having already secured their dates for the weekend—there was something else disturbing going on.

Jenna, the bride-to-be, had called. She wanted to have dinner with them tonight.

"Why?" Nola had instantly asked. She'd never liked Jenna much. Perhaps it was because she was a whiner used to get her own way all the time. Or was it because Jenna's father loved her beyond compare and spared no expense in proving that fact? Nola's deadbeat dad was somewhere between Virginia and New York where he'd managed to dodge child-support payments like Ron Isley dodged the IRS.

"I'm not sure, but she sounded a little strange," Cally said.

"Is that something new?" Nola said drily.

Serena laughed. "Not really, but since she's getting married in a few days we should probably take the time to meet with her. She may be having second thoughts."

"If she's got any sense at all she *is* having second thoughts," Nola said, staring contemplatively out the window in her bedroom. If Jenna called off the wedding she wouldn't have to continue the manhunt. Not that she'd been doing much in that regard anyway.

She'd been at a domestic hearing all Monday morning and then had a late lunch with one of the partners at the firm. She'd spent the remainder of her afternoon returning phone calls and e-mails until 5:30 had rolled around and she'd been so agitated by the staff and her clients that she'd packed her briefcase and came home to continue working.

That was quickly interrupted by the phone call from her cousins. And after she'd finally managed to get them and their I-got-some-today attitudes off the phone she'd been even more wound up and too distracted to work.

She hadn't slept well that night and had finally awakened at around 4:00 in the morning. Deciding sleep was futile at this point, Nola opted to take a shower and head into the office. If she got there before the staff arrived and before the phones started ringing she had no doubt she'd be able to get some work done.

Ten minutes later, very warm water, on the brink of scorching her skin, pounded against her body. Resting her forehead on the wall of the shower, Nola let the heated droplets attempt to relax her while her mind continued to wander. Ever since Friday night's plan of action was plotted she'd had a very unstable feeling.

It wasn't that she didn't believe herself attractive. No, that was clearly not the case. If nothing else, Nola had confidence in her looks and her professional capabilities. What she did not have confidence in were men. A long time ago she realized that was a result of her father abandoning her mother and his three-year-old daughter. And while logically she could say that he was young and stupid and that it was his loss, emotionally she'd carried the scars for the remaining thirty years of her life.

Nola had long since vowed to never let a man have that type of control over her emotions again. As such, she dealt with men sparingly and only in the sense of sexual gratification. Bruce was good to her, as were her fingers and her own imagination. But every once in a while she did get the urge to feel a long, hot dick deep inside her. Sometimes she needed the strength of a man thoroughly aroused ramming into her until she was completely drained.

Her body shook with the thought.

She turned to face the shower nuzzle, letting the water hit her breasts with pleasurable consistency. Her skin tingled and her pussy muscles began to contract.

She knew what that meant.

Cursing softly because Bruce was in her nightstand drawer, Nola contemplated whether to hurry up and wash and get out of the shower or to take the time to release this tension. She opted for the latter, convincing herself that her day would be much more productive if she did so.

Nola's life was carefully planned, her schedule very important to her. So allowing for impromptu sexual escapades wasn't always possible. Normally her time for pleasure was at night after a long bath, initiated by a glass of Chardonnay and topped off by Miles Davis's trumpet melodies lulling her to sleep.

This morning she would have to break from the norm.

Picking up the soap, she created a thick lather, then replaced the bar in its holder and began to rub her now aching breasts. Sensations rippled through her body with slow consistency beginning the dance of nerves and hormones deep inside her body. She leaned back against the wall of the shower letting her hands travel lower to her flat stomach down her hips, around to her butt.

Small sighs escaped as she imagined her hands were bigger, stronger, masculine. She squeezed her butt cheeks and moaned. Then she smacked the soap-soaked mounds and bit her bottom lip as essence seeped from her center. Deciding she liked the sound and feel of that action she repeated it, again and again.

By now her thighs were shaking, her pussy throbbing, a call to whatever she could find to insert inside to ease this need. She stepped under the water, letting it cascade over her skin while her breathing accelerated. Again her hand slipped over her breasts, stopping to tug the erect nipples, pulling them outward then letting them go; they bounced in resistance. She cupped the mounds and squeezed them until her nails began to penetrate her skin. She lifted them and extended her tongue, running moisture over the heavy swells then taking each nipple into her mouth for a thorough licking.

Her pussy spasmed and she groaned. She needed relief and she needed it now. Quickly her hands moved from her heaving breasts down past her stomach to her clean-shaved mons. Instinctively her thighs spread and her fingers slipped between the moist folds. She rubbed her clit, slipping aside the tight hood to toy with the bud until her entire body shook. That wasn't enough. Keeping one finger on her clit, another one slid into her hole, sinking into the cushiony softness of her vagina.

With lightning-fast strokes, because she still wanted to get to the office early, Nola pushed herself right over the cliff of ecstasy. And after a few moments to catch her breath she retrieved the soap again, washed up, and got out of the shower.

The office was quiet, thank the Lord, as Nola sat in her high-backed leather chair and clicked on her computer. On the ride into the office she'd decided to treat this date thing like a business deal. That was the best option. This way she wouldn't have to express the no-strings-attached rule. A professional would know they were only hired for a job and thus would have no problem walking away.

Signing on to the Internet, she typed in the name of a local dating service she only knew because her client's husband had found his mistress there and waited for the profile form to upload. Her cousins were prepared to pay a man with sex; well, she would pay him with a check on Sunday evening when she was safely back at her apartment in Baltimore.

Since Nola had never done anything like this before and because the profile form seemed to be quite in depth, she skipped it, opting to read a few of the entries first. She was reading about a very handsome businessman when the door to her office opened.

Nola glanced at the clock that read 6:15, then shifted her gaze to the door, to the person entering her office.

"I see we were both thinking alike this morning," a deep voice sounded. "Good morning, Nola."

Slowly Nola sat back in her chair and folded her hands in her lap. "Good morning, Mark. What can I do for you?" She wasn't real sure why he was in the office this early nor did she care, she simply wanted him gone as soon as possible.

Mark smiled and closed the door behind him before continuing his trek across the floor toward her desk. "Now that's a loaded question."

"It's a business question since we *are* in a place of business," Nola snapped. She didn't like Mark Riley.

"A lot of personal things have been known to happen in a place of business," he quipped.

Nola watched him closely. If she were in a better mood, and if she liked him, she would readily admit that Mark Riley was a very attractive man. He was at least six-foot-three, which matched perfectly with her five-foot-eleven stature. His shoulders were broad, his waist tapered, his thighs muscled. His skin tone was a creamy caramel with light brown eyes that almost seemed translucent at times. His lips were on the thick side, the top one covered with a neatly trimmed mustache. Yes, he was very attractive.

He was also a man.

And a law clerk—another one of the reasons why she didn't like him.

She sighed impatiently. "Not to me."

Mark unbuttoned his suit jacket and adjusted his pants before sitting in the chair across from her desk. "I missed you for dinner last night," he commented.

Nola heard him talking but her eyes were fastened to his big hands and flashbacks of the way she'd rubbed her breasts just an hour ago appeared. She'd squeezed and kneaded her skin with as much pressure as her thin female hands could muster. All the while craving for a heavier, more masculine touch. With much effort she lifted her gaze to his face.

"I never agreed to have dinner with you."

His hands remained on his thighs as he watched her. "I wish that you had."

"We've been over this before," Nola said, shifting in her seat in an attempt to dismiss the sudden heat forming between her thighs. "I am not going out with you."

Mark's grin was slow, his gaze intense as he spoke. "Because I'm a law clerk and you're a partner."

Nola nodded in agreement. "That, among other things."

"I'm also a man and you . . ." His eyes moved slowly, boldly from her face down to her breasts and rested there for a scorching moment before returning back to her face again. "And you are definitely a woman."

Nola's pussy clenched, an undeniable message that her earlier activities were not enough. He looked at her as if he could see right through her. She wasn't opposed to men looking at her. In fact, she enjoyed it. That's why she made sure her clothes fit her well, accenting every attribute she had. She didn't want a man but she had no problem with torturing them. Keeping that in mind, while trying to ignore the stirrings of desire, she crossed her legs and let her own jacket fall open.

"I know what I am, Mark. Just as I know what I do and do not want. I do not want to go out with you," she said matter-of-factly.

Mark shrugged. "That's fair."

She was momentarily shocked by his easy concession. For the last three months Mark had been asking her out. He was always polite, even charming at times, but he remained persistent. At least he had been. Today seemed to bring a different Mark entirely. Nola didn't know if she should be happy or hurt by that.

Finally she decided she didn't care either way. "Is there something else you wanted?" Nola had more pressing matters on her mind than trying to figure out a man she wasn't interested in anyway. Finding a date for the weekend was a priority.

"Yes." Mark continued to eye her steadily. "I had a question and since I know you are a woman of integrity and great confidence I know you'll have no problem responding honestly."

If she were prone to flattery Nola probably would have blushed and thanked him profusely. But since she didn't believe a word the man said she simply arched a brow. "Proceed."

"Do you want to fuck me?"

Nola swallowed hard and had to clamp down on her restraint with all forces. No way had she been expecting him to ask her that and no way was she prepared to answer. But it was against her very being to be intimidated.

"I don't see the relevance in that question."

Mark chuckled. "The relevance lies in your answer."

Nola stood, smoothed down her skirt, and walked around the desk. "Discussing sexual encounters in the workplace is illegal. Even a law clerk should know that."

He looked her up and down in a bold, direct glare that made her feel naked, vulnerable. She'd long ago admitted that there was something about Mark Riley that intrigued her, if not frightened her just a bit. He was just as confident as she was, just as self-assured and arrogant. That shouldn't be a bad thing except that his confidence and arrogance had a darker edge, an aura that she was afraid would easily overpower her.

And if, coupled with those feelings and the fact that they worked together wasn't conflict enough, she was turned on by him, by his lips, his dark, seductive eyes and his muscular build. He exuded an air of power and sexuality that completely aroused her. She'd tried to hide it with smart retorts and adamantly refusing to go out with him, but now that they were alone in her office she felt her defenses weakening.

Mark licked his lips. Nola's breath hitched as she visual-

ized him licking her pussy lips with that same slow precision. Her juices dripped down her thighs until she feared
she'd leave a puddle on the floor.

"I tried to take the honorable route and you shot me
down repeatedly. I finally figured out that I needed to ap-
proach you on your level." He stood and looked down at
her.

He was close enough for her to smell his cologne but
too far away for her to touch. That bothered her so she
took a step forward. "And asking me that question was on
my level?"

Mark copied her action so that they now stood only an
inch or two apart. "Yes, but you haven't answered me yet.
Shall I ask again?"

Because she liked to watch his mouth move, liked to
imagine those sensual lips exploring her intimately, she
said, "Yes, maybe you should."

Mark took another step until her breasts brushed
against his chest. Nola didn't move although every nerve
in her body stood immediately on end.

"Do . . . you . . . want . . . to . . . fuck . . . me?"

With each word he enunciated came a strong pulsating
in her pussy. She could lie and act insulted. She could
throw him out of her office and possibly have him fired
and prosecuted on sexual harassment charges.

Or . . .

She could jump on her desk, spread her legs, and let
him fuck her senseless. Each option held its own level of
satisfaction, the latter being most fascinating.

"Yes," she finally answered. "I do." Again, she was not
about to be intimidated by him. She was a grown woman
with needs, one of which was to be fucked by this most intriguing and challenging man.

Mark's smile spread and he reached a hand out to

squeeze her tender breast. She inhaled deeply, having already imagined the feel of his strong hands on her. Her mind was already made up, but she would not make it easy for him. Besides, the chase was turning her on. "But I won't."

His hand stilled, his smile slipping slightly. "You will."

She liked the feel of him touching her, that wasn't the issue, so she covered his hands and squeezed tighter. "No. I won't."

"I want to make you come," he admitted through clenched teeth. "I want to control your pleasure."

That was precisely what she was afraid of. "Nobody controls me," she said in a breathy whisper, still guiding his hand to knead her breast as she desired.

He pulled his hand away from her in a gesture so rough it caused her to take a step back.

"We'll see about that," he said.

Nola didn't know what to expect. Mark's light eyes had darkened and in a split second he'd gone from the smiling law clerk who obviously had a crush on her to a man very aroused by the idea of having sex with her. She was both intrigued and turned on.

She was also surprised when he grabbed her by the waist and turned her around, pulling her roughly against his body. One hand cupped her mound while the other cupped her breast. "I will control you and your pleasure and you won't try to stop me."

"That would be classified as rape and is punishable by twenty-five years in jail," she hissed even though her panties were growing wetter by his forceful fondling.

"No. It's not rape," he said, grounding his thick erection into her back. "You want it as much as I want to give it to you."

"You have no idea what I want." However, he was doing a pretty good job of finding out.

It only took a step forward to have her thighs pressed against the rim of the desk and a jerk of his hand to have her skirt up and around her waist. He pulled back the hand that had cupped her mound, lifting it to his mouth, where he thoroughly licked his fingers before slipping his hand beneath her panty hose. She felt his damp fingers parting her butt cheeks, easing down her crease, pausing at her anus.

"You think I don't know what you want?" he growled in her ear a mere second before pushing his forefinger past the puckered skin into her delectable tightness.

Nola moaned and pumped back against his hand. "I didn't say I wanted that," she panted.

"Then say it or I'll stop."

Nola remained quiet and his finger stilled. The pressure remained, the steady building of pleasure paused midstream and she moaned. His finger filled her but not nearly as much as she wanted it to, needed it to. "I want it," she conceded and he continued.

Nola leaned forward on the desk, planting her palms on the cool cherrywood for leverage. Mark finger-fucked her with a force driven only from a deep-seated desire and Nola pumped with him.

"Come for me."

Nola shook her head negatively even though she knew the volcano raging inside was destined to erupt . . . soon. "No. I won't give you anything."

Quickly he pulled his hand out of her, pushed her stockings and panties down in one motion. Spreading her cheeks wide, he sank to his knees. "Oh, yes you will," he growled before licking her from her anus, to her pussy hole, to her clit.

Nola's legs shook as his tongue continued to invade her with long, tortuous strokes then deep, languorous thrusts.

On and on he licked and sucked her pussy while she was sprawled over her desk. He pushed her legs apart, spreading her wider, getting an unadulterated view of her treasure. Mark rolled her clit between his fingers, then sucked on it gently. His tongue pierced her hole until she heard the moist sound of his entrance and retreat echoing throughout the room.

He sounded hungry, growling and moaning as he engorged on her body, her essence. When she tried to move, to back up against his mouth, a hand to the small of her back stopped her, held her completely still. Pulling his tongue out of her center, Mark licked back toward her anus then forward to her hole again and again.

Nola's moans grew louder and she knew that no matter what she'd said, what her brain had refused to do, her body was about to contest.

When Mark's fingers slipped into her ass and his tongue thrust into her center again she screamed, letting the most intense orgasm she'd ever experienced invade her body and escape with a flush of fluids that he seemed to savor.

"So did you ask him to come with you this weekend?" Cally said while spreading butter over her roll.

Nola gulped the white Zinfandel the waitress had just set in front of her. Placing the empty glass none too gently on the table, she sighed. "No. I didn't get a chance to ask him anything."

"What about after he made you come all over your desk?" Serena propped her elbows up on the table and smiled giddily.

"Don't be crass," Nola scolded.

Serena straightened in her seat. "Okay. Did you ask him after he'd eaten your pussy?"

"Serena!" Nola screamed.

Cally laughed and chewed on her bread. She loved the rolls at Phillip's Seafood Restaurant at the Inner Harbor.

"Oh come on, Nola, stop acting like you have virgin ears. Where was that snide attitude when you were letting the law clerk suck you dry? All I'm saying is after you finished the act—which sounds absolutely divine, by the way—why didn't you talk to him about the wedding?"

"I don't know," Nola said and let her head fall in her hands. "I was too baffled about what had just taken place to think about the wedding or anything else sane, for that matter."

"How come you haven't mentioned this guy before?" Cally asked.

"Because he's nobody," Nola answered quickly.

Serena shook her head negatively. "You let nobody make you come? That doesn't sound like you, Nola. What's really going on?"

Nola sighed heavily then signaled the waitress and waited until she came and took her order for another drink. When her new drink arrived she took a slower sip and sat back in her chair. "His name is Mark Riley. He's been there about six months and he's been asking me out for three months. I turned him down because I'm not interested."

Cally gave Nola a small smile. "That's a bit contradictory now, don't you think?"

"I know. I know." Nola groaned. "I just don't know how this happened. I mean, I went to work early to get some work done—"

"I'd say you got a lot accomplished," Serena interrupted.

Nola gave her an evil glare. "I had no idea he would be there. Besides, like I said, I'd been turning down all his offers. You know I'm not going out with a law clerk."

"You're not going out with anybody," Serena offered.

Cally reached across the table to take Nola's hand, partly because Nola looked as if she were about to wring Serena's neck if she made another comment. "It's okay, Nola. Being a law clerk is not like having some deadly disease. He's probably a pretty nice guy. At least you know he can please you before you've wasted your time going out with him."

Nola remembered back to early this morning, to the half hour she and Mark had spent alone in her office. She crossed her legs, clenching her pussy as tightly as possibly to ease the ache. That ache had been there since 7:30 this morning when Mark had smiled and wiped her essence from his face then told her to have a good day. How the hell did he expect her to have a good day after what he'd done to her?

"I'm still not going out with him," she said adamantly.

"Even though you agree that you've never been eaten out like that before?" Serena asked, then held up a hand to stop Nola's inevitable retort. "I'm just saying that maybe you should think twice about letting this one get away. I mean, you don't have to marry him, but there's no reason why you can't enjoy him."

"I have to agree with, Serena," Cally said. "You still need a date for the weekend. He's feeling you, that's obvious. And whether or not you're willing to admit it, you're kind of feeling him too."

"I am not feeling him," Nola said.

Serena rolled her eyes. "Just make pretend he has a law degree and invite him over to your house tonight. Fuck him and then ask him to spend the weekend with you. Damn, you're taking this way too seriously. I'm shocked."

Truth be told, Nola was shocked herself. All day long she'd been thinking about Mark, about his lips, his hands, and that huge erection he'd been sporting when he walked out of her office. She didn't like him, yet she wanted him like nobody's business. She'd thought he'd at least call her some time during the day, if not return to her office. But he'd done neither. That ticked her off even more than these desirous feelings she had that she couldn't seem to soothe herself.

She was about to explain this to her cousins when she looked up and saw Jenna heading for their table. Nola lifted a brow. Her younger cousin looked way too stressed to be getting married in four days.

"Hey, Jenna." Nola waved.

Jenna Barrett took the only available seat left at the table. "Hey," she said wistfully. "Thanks for meeting with me on such short notice."

Cally observed her younger cousin as she placed her purse on the side of the chair and fiddled with the napkin until she had it sitting in just the right position on her lap. Jenna was a pretty girl. Cally couldn't help but refer to her that way since she was almost eight years older than her. She had wavy dark blond hair, a creamy beige complexion, and wide hazel eyes. Eyes that today looked as if she'd just attended a funeral.

"You sounded like you really needed to talk. Are you okay?" Cally asked.

Jenna sighed heavily. "I'm fine, I guess."

"Girl, you don't look fine at all," Serena said bluntly. "Did something happen between you and Eddie?" Edward Remington was the man, twenty years Jenna's senior, that she was about to marry.

"Did you change your mind about getting married?" Nola asked hastily. "Because you know it's not too late."

"Nola!" Serena screeched.

"What?" Nola stared at Serena's appalled look and then

to Cally's questioning one. "It's not too late if she wants to change her mind. She shouldn't be rushed into this."

"It's not that," Jenna said in a small voice.

"Then what is it?" the threesome asked in unison.

Jenna looked startled for a moment, then she reached for Cally's glass of water and took a long swallow. "I'm pregnant."

Silence fell over the table like a heavy blanket.

"Well . . . that's a good thing, right?" Cally finally broke the silence.

Jenna tried to speak again but instead began to cry.

Nola sighed and snatched the napkin from Jenna's lap and dabbed at her eyes. "What are you crying for? You're getting married and you're starting a family. Isn't that what you planned?" The whole situation gave Nola the shivers but she didn't say that. Jenna looked as if she were about to crumble at any minute.

"I don't . . ." Jenna hiccupped, and took a deep breath. "I don't know if Eddie will be happy."

Cally sighed with relief while Serena sat back in her chair and said, "Girl, please, a man his age is bound to be happy that he can still make a baby."

Cally cast a warning glance then shook her head. "Have the two of you discussed children yet?"

Jenna shook her head negatively. "No."

"Do you even want a baby?" Nola asked because she was skeptical about this whole affair. According to her mother, Jenna had met Edward Remington, an oil magnate approaching his forty-eighth birthday, just a little over four months ago. Eddie had used his money and his influential status in the shoreside town of St. Michael's to woo Jenna. This hadn't been a terribly difficult feat since Jenna was fresh out of culinary college with wide eyes, a giddy nature, and a buxom figure that older men played on. In the span of three weeks Jenna had moved into Eddie's estate before going off to London with him for a six-week excursion. For the next month Eddie kept Jenna even closer, taking her to high-society parties and business conventions, preparing her for the job of trophy wife. Then he'd popped the question and the rest is history.

Sure, the story sounded blissfully romantic, but Nola suspected something else was going on.

"Is this why you agreed to marry him because you're carrying his baby?" Nola asked with a lifted brow.

"No, Nola!" Jenna raised her voice for the first time since entering the restaurant. "What type of woman do you think I am?"

Nola shrugged. "Obviously a very confused one."

"Nola, that's not fair. Jenna's facing a lot of changes in a short span of time. It's understandable that she'd be a bit emotional," Cally chided.

"I told you she was too young to get married," Serena added to Cally and nodded to Nola.

"I agree," Nola said begrudgingly. It was rare that her and Serena agreed on anything.

Jenna slammed a hand down on the table. "I am a grown woman. I know what I want and I'm getting married." When nobody bothered to say another word she wiped her eyes, lifted her menu, and said, "Now let's eat."

CHAPTER FOUR

A riotous rainbow of colors blossomed in front of Cally as she opened the door to her apartment. Smiling at the distinct smell of fresh flowers she leaned against the door frame waiting for the bearer of the floral creation to appear.

"The florist said that these were sure to please. Orange Asiatic lillies, belladonna delphiniums, liatris, yellow snaps, and burgundy *Matsumoto* asters, all wrapped in these leafy things and this noisy, but festive, green paper," Steven recited as he peeked from behind the flowers. His broad smile caused Cally's heart to skip a beat.

She warmed all over, a feeling that was foreign to her. "You can tell the florist that I am very pleased." Taking the flowers from him, she inhaled their sweet scent. "They smell so nice. Come on in."

Cally heard the door close behind her and headed for the kitchen. Steven watched her as she walked; she knew because she could feel the heat of his gaze moving down

her back, caressing her bottom and stroking her legs. She
tightened her grip on the flowers and called over her
shoulder, "Have a seat. I'm just going to get a vase and I'll
be right out."

She was already in the kitchen when she heard him
murmur some type of response. His words did not have to
be audible for Cally to react. It had always been the rich,
deep timbre of his voice that turned her on first. Although, since their intimate appointment in his office two
days ago, Cally had been aroused 24-7. That was strange,
even for her. She loved sex but she'd never thought about
it as much as she did now since having a taste of Steven—
or should she say the taste he had of her.

Actually, he'd been the only one getting a taste. He'd
held her captive on that table for what seemed like hours,
but was more like twenty long, fantastic minutes. After lap-
ping up her third orgasm he told her he had an appointment and they'd have dinner to discuss her need of a
date. Cally had been too shaky to argue that he could just
answer her right then and get it over with, so she'd agreed.
The date hadn't been able to take place last night since
Jenna was in need of some womanly companionship. But
all day long she'd thought of seeing the good doctor again
tonight.

He was in the living room, only a few feet away from her
and she felt her legs trembling in response. Memories of
being on that examining table with his mouth locked between her legs made *horny* seem like a virginal word in her
vocabulary. Grasping the counter for balance, she tried to
focus her thoughts. Steven was a serious man. She could
tell by the ease in which he'd risen from between her legs,
moved to the tiny sink in the room, and rinsed her
essence from his face and mouth. He'd turned to her ca-
sually and rattled off dinner plans like it was etched in

stone, then he'd smiled and left her there. She'd been still sitting on the table, her wet pussy throbbing and open for all to see.

Yesterday she'd had a chance to really think about the doctor and what she was doing with him. She'd decided there was nothing to think about. They were attracted to each other, which turned out to be a good thing since she wanted him to go to St. Michael's with her for the weekend. He was intelligent, which was another plus because at least they could have real conversations in between the hot sex. And he was a professional. She liked a man with dedication to his career, that way he had no issues about her dedication to hers.

Still, it was just a weekend gig for Cally. She would most likely need to find herself a new GYN now, but she didn't really mind. After this week she would have had Dr. Steven Bradford in every way, shape, and form, thus satisfying her thirst for him. First thing Monday morning she would get back to work on the article she hadn't touched since coming home from the doctor's earlier this week.

"I can't tell you the last time a guy brought me flowers," Cally said as she returned to the living room, setting the vase full of flowers on the coffee table. She nuzzled the buds again before turning to face him.

"I'm glad you like them. This is a nice place you have here," he commented, looking around the room.

"Thanks," Cally said then took a seat on the sofa next to him. "Do you live in the city?"

"Yes. I live in the condos near Johns Hopkins. I did my residency there and wanted to be close."

"Oh? I'm surprised."

He looked at her quizzically. "You are? Why?"

"I just pictured you owning your own home. A big colonial in Harford County someplace."

Steven chuckled. "I'm not sure if I should be offended or not."

"Don't be offended. I didn't mean anything bad. It's just that you look accomplished and focused and all together." She shrugged when she couldn't quite explain what she was trying to say.

"I do own my condo and I am accomplished and focused. But I'd like to wait until my wife can choose our home with me."

There it was. Cally almost sighed. He had a wife. She'd slept with married men before. Men whose wives didn't seem to be keeping the home fires burning but for whatever reasons, those seemed to be the hardest affairs to break. You would have thought since they had a prior commitment it would be easy, but married men seemed to cling a little more than she liked.

That's why in the last two years she'd sworn off married men. That and the fact that she was getting tired of sharing. While she wasn't ready to commit to a man forever, she at least wanted his undivided attention for the duration of their affair.

"So is your wife out looking for your new home tonight?" she asked with a definite bite to her words. Dr. Bradford had been a good prospect for what she needed, but now she was going to have to cuss him out and send him packing.

"No," he answered calmly, then reached for her hand. "I haven't found my wife yet."

It took her a minute to realize that he'd placed her hand on top of his left one. She looked down and noticed there was no ring.

"I see," she said simply. "That's a relief."

Steven entwined his fingers with hers and smiled. "Do you really think a married man would do the things I did to you the other day?"

She chuckled. "I know they would."

Steven lifted a brow and stared at her. Cally just shook her head. "Don't ask and I won't tell."

He grinned. "Fair enough. So you ready to go to dinner?"

"We're really going to dinner?" she asked.

"Of course. I told you that before you left the office."

"I thought that was just your way of getting to my apartment," she said honestly. She'd dressed in a short black skirt and wraparound red top but hadn't bothered with underwear because—with the exception of Drake—when a guy said that he was picking her up for dinner they normally ended up naked on the living room floor, having dessert in her kitchen a couple of hours later.

He stared at her intently, so much so that she'd become uncomfortable and tried to pull away, but he held her hand tighter. "If I wanted to come to your apartment to have sex with you, that's what I would have said. I say what I mean, Calathia, and I mean what I say."

And what you say makes me damned wet, she thought, as she shifted her thighs to keep the growing moisture between her legs at bay. "Call me Cally," she said quietly.

Steven lifted her hand to his lips and brushed a light kiss over her knuckles, then turned it palm-up and circled his tongue over the center. "I'm taking you to dinner, Cally."

She licked her lips, unable to find a response.

"We'll have sex later," he said, grinning.

Cally smiled in return. "I'll just bet we will."

When they pulled up in front of Outback Steakhouse, Cally couldn't contain her look of surprise.

"What? You don't like steak?" Steven asked and helped her out of the car.

"I do. I, um, I'm just surprised that this is the place you'd take me on our first date."

Steven held her hand as they walked across the parking lot. "Not high-class enough for you? Not expensive enough?" he asked with a smile.

"I'm not a gold digger, if that's what you're hinting at. This just doesn't seem like a place you frequent much."

Steven opened the door and held it while she walked in ahead of him. "You seem to have had a lot of preconceived ideas about me. I eat here at least once a week. Their bread is awesome."

Cally smiled. For all that Steven looked uptight and serious, he was really easy to be around. During the ride over they'd developed a great rapport. The closer they became in the next couple of days, the more convincing they'd be at the wedding.

They were seated and munching on warm chunks of bread covered with butter, Cally's one weakness, when Steven spoke.

"Tell me more about this date you need?"

Cally finished chewing and wiped her hand on a napkin. "My cousin is getting married on Sunday. I need a date to go to St. Michael's with me for the wedding."

He nodded. "You have family in St. Michael's?"

"Yes. All of my family lives there except for me and my other two cousins. We were the rebels of the clan. As soon as we graduated high school we made a beeline to the city for college."

"You mean you headed to the city to find boys," Steven chuckled.

Cally angled her head and smiled. "How did you know?"

"You are very sure of your effect on men, Cally. That tells me you've been practicing for a really long time."

Cally laughed. "If you say so. Anyway, I don't want to go back home alone."

"But your other two cousins are going with you?"

"We're three peas in a pod. Always have been and probably always will be. Nola, Serena, and I are the three surviving single women of our generation. That fact causes a lot of discussion whenever we go home."

"So you think if you take a date home with you it'll ease some of the talk?"

She nodded. "I hope so."

Steven took another bite of bread and stared at her contemplatively.

"So will you go with me? It's for the whole weekend. I know it's short notice but . . ."

"But you just decided to ask me after what happened on Monday," he finished for her.

Their appetizer arrived and Cally grinned. Besides her sexuality there was only one other thing that Cally did not bother to deny—her appreciation of food. It was a wonder she was able to maintain her fit size-ten body, but then she also had a personal trainer who would have a cow if he saw her hastily reaching for the blooming onion sitting on the table between her and Steven.

Steven didn't waste time digging in, either, and it was a few moments before she could speak again.

"I actually decided to ask you the night before the appointment."

"Really?" He arched a brow.

How did he manage to look so intellectual yet so tasty at the same time? "Yes, really. I've been seeing you for about two years now and I've noticed how good-looking you are. What better way to fool my parents into thinking I'm finally settling with one man then by bringing home a gorgeous doctor?" She grinned.

Steven's expression grew serious. "So are you finally settling on one man or are you just looking for a date for the
weekend?"

A piece of onion lodged in her throat and Cally began
to cough. Steven was at her side, instantly rubbing her
back. When she'd stopped coughing he lifted her glass of
water to her lips and held it while she sipped. Cally
cleared her throat again and nodded to him that she was
all right. But instead of him taking that as his cue and returning to his seat, he scooted her aside and sat next to
her.

"Shall I ask the question again?" he said, reaching for
another piece of the onion.

"No. I heard you the first time." She cleared her throat
again, not because anything was stuck in it this time, but
to stall for a few more minutes. Cally wasn't certain, but
she had a feeling that Steven wasn't going to like her answer. She wondered if that would make him change his
mind about going with her, if he was even considering it.
Deciding that he wasn't the only man she could ask—but
was the one she preferred—she answered him. "I'm not
ready to settle down. Unfortunately, my mother thinks
that my biological clock is ticking and that I should put a
little pep in my step. So to answer your question, yes, the
date is just for the weekend."

Steven didn't comment.

"Will you go with me?"

He turned to look at her. "You've got some cheese on
your lip."

Cally reached for a napkin, but he stilled her hand.
Leaning closer, his tongue extended and he licked the
crevice of her lip until the cheese was gone. "I'd love to
spend the weekend with you, Cally," he whispered against
her lips.

*   *   *

"Stop calling me!" Jenna yelled into her cell phone. She was driving down the winding road leading from Eddie's house. Her mother and her aunts were meeting her and her bridal party for a day at the spa.

"How can you marry him, Jenna? You told me you loved me?"

He'd been calling her regularly since the last time she'd seen him about a month ago. She'd told him it was over, had written him a letter, and met him in person to end their affair. And yet he continued to call. This couldn't go on. Eddie would kill him if he found out about their affair and Jenna had no idea what Eddie would do to her.

Not to mention the wedding that was about to take place. Three hundred invitations that had gone out, the church rented, the caterer paid, flowers ordered, and so on and so on. And then there were her parents and the rest of her family that were so proud her heart broke each time she continued to lie to them. There was too much at stake. Too much to throw away for a few months of good sex.

"They were just words. Words spoken in the heat of the moment. Men do it all the time," she sighed and tried to focus on the road.

"You meant it, Jenna. I know you meant them. You should be marrying me."

"No. I'm marrying Eddie and that's final. Now I would advise you to stop calling me. It's not going to be good for either of us if you don't."

He was quiet so long Jenna thought he'd hung up, but then he spoke and her blood froze.

"It's not going to be good for any of us, anymore."

*   *   *

Nola had no idea what she was doing or why she was doing it. The note said to meet him here, at this hotel, at this time.

When she'd returned from lunch earlier this afternoon it had been taped to her computer screen, with the cryptic message scrawled in almost illegible writing. At first she crumpled it and tossed it in the trash can. About an hour later, because she'd been unable to think of anything else, she retrieved it and reread it. For the next three hours she'd reread it a dozen times wondering what it meant and if she even wanted to find out.

At 5:00 her curiosity got the best of her and she switched off her computer and went home to shower and change. It was now 6:25; she was five minutes early, and she was at the Marriott Waterfront Hotel, on the fifth floor about to knock on this door and continue what they'd started in her office yesterday.

She'd finally come to the conclusion that since she'd answered Mark's question he planned to call her on her honesty. She admitted she wanted him to fuck her and she assumed that's what he planned to do.

Shivers ran up and down her spine as she knocked on the door, anticipation a powerful aphrodisiac.

He answered the door almost instantly and Nola resisted the urge to smile. He looked good dressed in black slacks and a black silk shirt that didn't begin to button until mid-chest. That left a sexy peek of dark hair on his chest, hair that Nola wanted to run her fingers through.

"Punctual as well as beautiful," he said, smiling, then moved to the side to allow her entrance.

"I have other things to do so whatever it is you wanted I'd like to get it over with as quickly as possible." Even the simple act of walking had her aroused. She wore a thong beneath her slacks so her bare bottom rubbed against the poly-cotton material, causing friction that only height- ened her sense of arousal. The fact that she was in a hotel room, alone, with the very sexy law clerk that had brought her a tremendous climax yesterday probably had some- thing to do with it as well.

"I thought we could spend some time together. You know, get to know each other."

His smile was deadly, a mixture of pure sex appeal and boyish charm.

She faced him and crossed her arms over her chest. "What is it you'd like to know about me? You've already figured out the most important thing."

"And that is?"

"How to make me scream."

His smile widened and he moved to stand in front of her. "I already knew how to do that."

His fingers raked through her chin-length hair and he grasped her head, pulling her closer. "Now I want to show you how you can make me holler."

Her mouth watered; still Nola pulled away from his grasp. "For the record, I'm well-versed on bringing men to their knees. So I don't need a lesson from you." She walked over to the couch, knowing he'd follow her. "But if that's what this visit is truly about then I want something in return, before I pleasure you."

As she'd expected, he followed her to the couch and paused at her words. "You're a lawyer, not a prostitute. What could you possibly want in return?"

"I need a date," she said simply.

He chuckled. "What? I thought you said you didn't want to go on a date with me."

"I didn't. And I'm not admitting to wanting to go on a date with you. I said I *need* a date. There's a difference."

"There is? Explain it to me," he said, taking a seat on the sofa then patting the cushion beside him for her to do the same.

Nola sat, making sure to be close to him but not touch him. He hadn't tried to hide his erection and she hadn't tried not to look at it. But she wasn't ready for him just yet.

"I need a date for a wedding I'm invited to in St. Michael's. I'm leaving Friday evening and I'm returning Sunday evening. I don't need or want a boyfriend or anything beyond this weekend. Are you game?"

Mark continued to smile, a grin that insinuated that he knew what she was thinking. And when his hand moved from his knee to grip the bulge in his pants she realized he *did* know what she was thinking.

"I'm game. Are you?"

Procrastination was not one of Nola's traits. However, she did like things to take place on her time, by her rules.

She stood and pulled her blouse from the rim of her pants and over her head. "I'm game." Her high breasts stood erect and she watched as his gaze fell to their tightened peaks. "This is over on Sunday. Understood?"

Mark continued massaging his erection and nodded. "But I'm going to thoroughly enjoy myself until then."

CHAPTER FIVE

"Suck it harder," Mark groaned, his fingers twisted in Nola's hair as he fucked her mouth.

Nola heard him and was encouraged, taking him in deeper, until the crown of his dick touched the back of her throat. She sucked him harder, just as he requested, hollowing her cheeks on the upstroke.

She lay on the king-sized hotel bed, his knees planted on each side of her face, his hands buried in her hair. Nola opened her eyes and saw his powerful hips pumping toward her face, felt his huge balls slapping against her chin.

He'd thought he was the only one who could make a person scream. Well, from the looks of him now—the way his strong jaw clenched, his lips thinned out, his breath hissed through his teeth, his eyes rolled back in his head—she'd say he'd be screaming in just about two seconds.

Undressed, Mark was even bigger than she'd imagined. Muscles rippled from every possible part of his body, from the bulging veins in his neck to the tight bounce of his ass. He was a gorgeous specimen and she was determined to take as much of him as she could.

Grabbing the base of his dick she guided him in and out, controlling the depth and pressure of each thrust. Her pussy pulsed to the rhythm of her mouth around his enlarged piece. Cream filled her center and she opened her legs instinctively, wishing she could reach around his thick form to finger herself while she brought him pleasure.

As if he sensed her need, Mark slowly pulled out of her mouth, gasping as her teeth raked over his turgid length. She knew her lips were glistening with the same moisture that coated his dick but didn't bother to wipe them as she glared up at him. "Where are you going? I wasn't finished."

"Don't worry," he said, grinning down at her, "I'm coming back."

And that he did, after he turned so that his large dick pistoned into her mouth from another direction. Strong hands pushed her thighs apart and the hot flat of his tongue covered her aching pussy.

Nola sighed as he pumped his length into her mouth again, his testicles brushing over her nose. He continued to lick her pussy in long, slow motions until she thought she would scream with need for more. Again, he knew what she needed without her having to say a word, not that she could when her mouth was full to overflowing with his huge endowment.

Reaching his hands around to her rear, Mark spread her butt cheeks wide, finding her puckered anus and breach-

ing the tight hole. His tongue sank into her drenched
pussy and he matched the rhythm threefold—his finger in
her ass, his tongue in her pussy, his dick in her mouth.

Nola feared she'd be the one screaming before long.

It seemed they went on like that, pleasuring each other
for hours and hours then Mark's vigorous movements in
her mouth became stilted as if he were trying to hold on
but steadily losing the battle. At that very same moment
Nola felt a clenching in the pit of her stomach, a tightening in her core that increased with each downward thrust
of his dick in her mouth. With one hand she grabbed his
large member at the base, pulling him down faster and
faster into the moist recess of her mouth. Her other hand
found his swollen testicles, kneading the tight sac until
she felt his muscled butt cheeks tightening.

Below she clenched her pussy muscles around his tongue.
He slipped the finger that had pumped her ass up past
her perineum toward her pussy and back, dragging her
juices down to her anus where his finger again slipped
into her tightness. Her entire body convulsed with the
sensation and she knew one major orgasm was on the way.

His mouth paused over her pussy the second the first
drop of hot cum landed in her mouth. His finger moved
with lightning speed in her ass, then his tongue returned
to flatten beneath the hood of her clit.

Nola couldn't scream with her release, instead she
squeezed his butt and swallowed his powerful release. Between her legs Mark did exactly the same.

Moments passed in silence as their breathing steadied,
then Mark turned and came to join her at the top of the
bed. He dropped a quick kiss on her forehead before
rolling onto his back beside her.

For a second Nola felt the sting of not being cuddled
after sex, which was weird because she'd never longed for

that intimacy before. And in retrospect this was not sex. He hadn't penetrated her . . . wait a minute, he had penetrated her mouth and her ass. Still, if his dick didn't get into her pussy, she hadn't had sex with him. That was her mantra and she was sticking to it.

And was this really intimate, she thought in defense of that one weird reflection that had surfaced. She'd arrived and within minutes stripped. He'd followed suit and stuck his dick in her mouth. She sucked him off and he sucked her off, that was it. Now they lay in the same bed but no part of their bodies touched. This was exactly the kind of interludes she preferred. Or so she thought.

"So what time are we leaving on Friday?" Mark asked.

"Seven," Nola answered after a moment of thought. "I don't want to get caught in vacationers' traffic."

"Good idea. I'll meet you at your place at six-thirty."

He didn't wait for a response but was off the bed and headed into the bathroom, leaving Nola to stare at his naked form as he did. Seconds later she heard the shower switch on and wondered if she should join him. He'd closed the door behind him, which demolished any thought of an invitation. Nola shrugged and slipped out of the bed, walking naked into the other room to retrieve her purse.

Finding her cell phone, she hit speed dial number three and waited for an answer. "Hey, it's me," she said in response to Cally's cheerful hello.

"Hey, what's up?"

"I found a date, so you can call Serena and tell her the plan is in full effect."

"Really? Who is he? Is it the law clerk?"

Nola rolled her eyes skyward; for women who didn't want to get married Cally and Serena were such romantics. "Yes, it's the law clerk. And no, we didn't go out on a

date. We did what was necessary to seal our deal and that's
all." The words sounded shallow and cold to her own ears
but she didn't care. It was what it was.

On the other end Cally laughed and Nola could even
hear her clapping her hands. "We are going to have such
a good time. I'm really looking forward to this weekend
now."

"Well, good for you. I still don't want to be bothered but
I don't really have a choice."

"Everything is going to work out, Nola. By the way, I
talked to Jenna again."

"Yeah? Has she changed her mind?" Nola could only
hope.

"No. But she still doesn't sound good. And my mother
called me a little while ago and said Jenna seemed really
distracted. The aunts think it's just nerves but I'm not so
sure. This pregnancy thing is really bothering her."

"It would bother me too if I were having a baby by someone old enough to be my father." Nola heard the shower
switch off and said, "Look, I gotta go. Call me at home
later."

Disconnecting the phone, she tossed it back into her
purse then returned to the bedroom where Mark was just
stepping out of the bathroom. That gorgeous body of his
flexed and profiled as he strutted across the room and
began putting on his clothes. He hadn't looked up at her
nor said a word so Nola quickly averted her gaze and
scooped her own clothes up before heading to the bathroom.

"Stop by my place tomorrow on your way to work, I've
got something for you to see."

Nola paused and glared at him. "You can stop bossing
me around. We have a deal so I plan to do my part but you
won't talk to me as if you're my superior."

Mark threw back his head and laughed. "You can be my superior in the office, Nola. I don't mind." He walked toward her and reached around to palm her ass. "But when we're alone I don't think there's any question who holds the control."

Cream pooled between her legs again but Nola would not visibly show how he weakened her. Instead, she cupped his now-flaccid penis, squeezing until it pulsed in her hand, signaling its compliance. "Control is such a funny thing, Mark. It can shift hands before you realize it."

He grinned and licked those sexy-ass lips. "Touché."

Nola released him after he'd pulled his hand away from her. "I'll be at your apartment at noon. I take an hour and a half for lunch so whatever you need to show me needs to fit into that time frame." This time she didn't wait for his response.

Serena was on a natural high Wednesday afternoon. She'd done the makeup for an up-and-coming singing group, garnering high praise from their manager and a promise to keep her in mind when the group went on their national tour. This came after the two dozen yellow roses were delivered to her apartment this morning with the card that said: *I love reminiscing with you.*

Yes, today was definitely a good day.

So as she stepped out of the high-rise condo building on Eutaw Street and gazed up at the sun shining brightly in the sky, she began to hum that tune again. The tune that she remembered playing in the background on the countless nights when two young adults lay in each other's arms making promises of forever. Instinctively she thought of James. Truth be told, he hadn't been far from her mind since the evening they'd spent at his apartment.

Serena readily admitted that the way James introduced

a stranger into their love life was sneaky and cause to
never forgive him, but that brief interlude had opened her
mind and an untapped sexual desire. Shortly after Sherry's
introduction, James had escorted the woman out. When
he returned it was only about him, only about Serena, about
the two of them, together again. Yet, she hadn't been able
to get the young woman out of her mind.

She smiled as she approached the crosswalk and the
traffic breezed by. When a car pulled close to the curb she
took a precautionary step backward. Then the back window came down and her smile spread wider.

"What are you doing here?"

James smiled from the backseat of the Lincoln Town
Car. "Picking my woman up from work." He stepped out
of the car and held the back door open for her. "Get in,"
he said.

Serena knew she had to look silly smiling brightly at this
man she'd known for years. But the smile was the only
thing holding the sentimental tears at bay. He'd called her
his woman. A part of her wanted to dispute his claim, to
remind him that she'd only agreed to seeing him again
for the sake of this wedding. Another part wanted to live
the fantasy as long as she could.

Sliding across the leather seat, she stopped at the passenger-side door and waited for James to get back in. "How
did you know where I was?" she asked when he'd closed the
door and motioned for the driver to continue.

"Cally told me," he said proudly. "It seems she's very excited about us being back together."

"Did you tell her we were back together?"

"I sure did. Why? Is that a problem?"

He'd scooted over until their sides were touching and
now was leaning in to kiss her ear, then that tiny spot beneath her lobe he favored.

"I didn't discuss that with her, that's all," she said quietly. Why wasn't she telling him they weren't back together? Why wasn't she setting him straight about this new arrangement?

"Now you don't have to."

His hand was on her thigh, squeezing in that way that said he wanted her to open for him. She did because to deny herself the illicit pleasure of his touch was insane.

"How was your day?" he whispered as his hand continued caressing her thigh, so that the material of her skirt began to gather.

It was the middle of the summer in Baltimore so stockings were a no-no in her book. The average daily temperature was ninety-eight degrees. So it wasn't long before James was caressing the bare skin of her thigh. In fact, it seemed like he was a breath away from her center only seconds after she'd climbed into the car. And that seemed perfectly normal. James picking her up from work and touching her intimately was like the sun rising and setting—it just was. Nobody ever questioned why, they just knew it would be. But then there were those rainy days.

"It was great," she said, still excited by the prospects, and refusing to let the other thoughts steal her joy. "Have you ever heard of Divine Destiny?"

James paused a moment, his lips still brushing against her neck, his thumb stroking her inner thigh. "I think I have. Why?"

"They had a photo shoot today and I did their makeup. The ladies were really pleased and their manager was also. He said he would definitely keep me in mind when they start touring in the fall."

James pulled back enough to look into her face then. His smile was slow and genuine and warmed Serena all the way down to her toes. "That's great, baby girl."

"I know. I'm pretty excited."

"Congratulations," he said, then leaned in, brushing his lips over hers.

Serena accepted the soft kiss and graciously slipped into the deeper melding of their tongues. Some people tended to underestimate the art of kissing. Serena and James did not.

Slowly his tongue moved across her lips. She sighed and opened her mouth to him, but he did not plunge inside. He stroked the bottom line of her teeth with his tongue, his lips not touching hers as he did. Then he stroked the top line. By that point Serena was almost begging for his tongue to mingle with hers, but she knew the drill.

She waited, holding her mouth only slightly ajar. He suckled her top lip, then moved to the bottom, pulling the swollen skin into his mouth as if he savored the very taste of her. Her hand came up around his neck, locking his head to hers. She tilted her head and extended her tongue to brush over his mustache-covered top lip. He groaned, one hand moving to her breast, the other pushing her thighs apart.

He released his hold on her lip and let the tip of his tongue touch the tip of hers. For endless moments their tongues twisted around each other, without the contact of their lips. He squeezed her nipple and Serena sighed, running her free hand along his chest.

Deft fingers slipped the crotch of her panties to the side, then slipped along her swollen center. It was at that moment that James allowed his lips to touch hers again. The contact was brief as he pulled back slightly and growled, "My lips."

He licked her bottom lip, simultaneously stroking the right side of her labia, then did the same with her top lip and the left labia.

Serena moaned in agreement.

His tongue entered her mouth and his finger slipped beneath her folds at the same time. He kissed her longingly while stroking her slowly. His touch was gentle on both ends, causing Serena to tense with anticipation. On and on the teasing seemed to go until she was squirming in the seat, her arousal oozing out onto her thighs. She was so wet the sound of his finger mingling with her juices echoed in the back of the car.

It was at that moment that Serena realized they weren't alone. She tried to close her legs and pushed on his chest.

"Please, baby girl, I love touching you like this," James moaned against her lips.

"But the driver," she warned.

"He's being paid to drive, not to watch us."

His tongue moved over her lips, down to her chin and to her neck where he bit lightly. His finger found her clit and stroked the tightened bud until she gasped.

"I need to taste you, Rena."

Serena's head had fallen back on the seat, thrashing side to side as ripples of pleasure coursed through her. "No, James. Not here."

"Please, baby girl," he sighed, nipping her breasts through the material of her blouse.

"James," she whimpered, knowing there was no use denying him.

A second later the car stopped.

"We're here, sir," a stern voice from the front seat said.

Serena jolted upright in her seat and James lifted his eyes to hers. He smiled. "So you're saved." He nipped her chin. "For the moment."

Serena rolled her eyes and began straightening her clothes. "Where are we?"

"I have a surprise for you," he said, then proceeded to

put his other hand up her skirt. "But first, we need to get rid of something."

"James?"

"Shhhh," he said, then looped his fingers in the band of her panties and pulled them down her legs.

"These are a major distraction." He smiled then stuffed them beneath the seat. "I'll get them when we come back."

Serena gave him an indignant glare. "I can't get out of this car with no underwear!"

He dropped a quick kiss on her lips. "Sure you can." The back door opened and he grabbed her hand, about to get out, then he turned back to her. "You can only do that when you're with me, Rena. If I ever hear of you parading around town without underwear and I'm not around to enjoy it you'll be severely punished."

Serena giggled. "And I'm so scared of you."

He squeezed her hand then got out of the car.

"Where are we?" Serena asked again when they were inside a building that looked like a warehouse.

"This is my building," James said before punching a code into a pad on the wall. "I purchased it a few months before I came back."

"So you've been planning to come back for a while? Why didn't you tell me?"

They'd taken a few steps to stand in front of double doors. James turned the knob and pulled the door open. A second later the wall beneath split and slid apart and they stepped into an elevator. When the doors closed and James pressed the button for the third floor he looked back at her and said, "I didn't want to come back into your life until my life was straight."

He looked serious, like he wasn't telling her everything.

That worried her. "What really happened in California, James? I don't understand why after seven years you just decided to come back home."

"I just did, Serena," he said simply.

And she knew for sure then that he was hiding something.

James led her down a long hallway. "The contractors will be finished in about two weeks." He let his hand glide along the stark white walls as they walked. "I was thinking of a gunmetal gray for the interior. What do you think?"

"What?" Serena hadn't really been paying attention to what he was saying, instead she'd been trying to figure out this change she sensed in him.

"The walls?" He turned to her. "You were talking about my apartment needing furniture but the studio takes precedence over that since this is where I'll be doing all my business from now on. What do you think of gray as the base of the color scheme?"

"Color scheme? What do you know about color schemes?" He was really confusing her now.

He chuckled. "I don't really, but I had a meeting with my decorator this morning and she was giving me all kinds of suggestions."

Then, as if for the first time since entering the building, realization dawned on her. "This is your studio?" She turned around, taking in the white walls, the few staggered doors toward the end of the hall, the emptiness. "I thought you were just going to write music from now on."

"I plan on writing and producing. I'm also thinking about having a management division that will scout local talent and create new stars."

Serena tilted her head and stared at him. "You've given this a lot of thought, I see."

James nodded and moved closer. "Yes. I have."

She backed away. Again, this was a new James she was seeing. He wasn't carefree and only concerned about singing anymore. The man in front of her seemed focused, matured, and ready to take on the world.

When she was trapped between the wall and James she looked away. If this were a new James then what they were doing wasn't reminiscing at all. It was something else, something dangerous, something she wasn't sure she would be able to handle after the weekend was over.

With his palms flat against the wall on either side of her face, James leaned in closer but did not touch her. "I've given you a lot of thought as well."

She still wouldn't look at him but felt the warmth of his breath on her forehead. Next she felt the tip of his finger against her chin, lifting her face to his.

"I've reevaluated what I want in my life, Rena."

"You have?" she asked in a shaky voice. Serena knew what she wanted in her life too. She wanted her job, she wanted to be a success. And once upon a time she'd wanted James Baker to marry her.

"Yes. I have."

Her back straightened as she reminded herself that when she'd expected a marriage proposal she'd received a good-bye. "And what have you decided you want, James?"

His finger drew lazy circles over her jaw, traced a slow line across her lips. Serena refused to tremble although her insides were already turning to mush.

"I want to make music during the day." His gaze fell to her mouth, his finger slowly parted her lips, slipped along the line of her teeth. "And I want to make love to you all night."

Serena shivered. She wouldn't suck his finger no matter how much she wanted to. She wouldn't close her eyes and take the digit into her mouth and imagine it was his dick. She wouldn't let herself fall into this clever little seduction because she was afraid that it would lead to so much more.

"That's fine for this week," she said, turning away from him again. "But what will you do after the wedding is over?"

James paused, looking as if she'd physically slapped him. He'd known coming home wasn't going to be easy and he'd sensed the hurt he'd caused Rena upon his return. He was young when he left, focused on his own goals, his own life. He hadn't thought about a future with her then because he hadn't been sure he could take care of her. Now things had changed. His life and his thinking had changed and he desperately wanted her to share that with him. But all she seemed to want was a date to this wedding. Or that's what she said.

"I'll deal with that when it gets here." He pushed closer to her, making sure she felt his rigid arousal against her belly. "For right now, I plan to enjoy making love to you as frequently as possible."

She squirmed against him and he settled in closer, leaned forward and bit her earlobe, then suckled the plump skin. "Did you really like Sherry, baby girl?" he whispered in her ear.

She sighed, tilting her head so he could have access to that spot beneath her ear he loved so much. He obliged, sucking the tender skin until he knew there would be a purple mark there when he finished.

"Tell me if you liked her, if you want her to join us again?"

"Yes, I liked her," she whispered.

He'd already been hot for her, already been hard enough to break through walls, but her admittance to liking the female sucking her pussy while he watched drove him insane. "What did you like most about her?" He palmed her breast, squeezing it as if he were milking her.

"I . . . I don't know," she stammered.

He pulled back and looked at her. Eyes darkened with desire, lips parted, breathing erratic, this was his Serena. This was the woman he had shared so much with, the woman who had given herself so completely to him, the woman he still loved. He would win her back. She would be his again, for now, for the weekend, for forever.

Dropping a chaste kiss on her forehead, he sighed. "We can talk about that later. I have something special for you." Clasping her hand, he pulled her from the wall and continued down the hallway to the last door on the end.

Once inside he switched on the light and closed the door behind them. "This is one of the recording studios. This floor is all studios, five in total. On the top floor are the business offices and downstairs will be the audition area."

"And the first floor?" Serena asked as she looked around at all the expensive equipment.

"The first floor will be general reception and I'm thinking about a hall of fame of sorts. To display all our acts and how well they're doing in their careers."

"Do you have groups already?"

"While I was in L.A. I made a lot of good contacts. I've written songs for a lot of major artists. So I'm constantly getting referrals and just last year one of the songs I wrote was nominated for a Grammy."

She smiled as she turned to face him. "Stop playing. Why didn't you call and tell me?"

"I did call you but you were out. I didn't leave a message because I wanted to talk to you personally. Then after I didn't win it, I just decided not to bother you at all."

"You decided not to call a lot, James."

The pain was clearly etched in her voice. He wouldn't deny it again. "Sit down," he said as he moved toward the sound board.

Surprisingly she did as he said, without much more than a quirk of a brow. He'd expected some smart retort about him bossing her around but none came. He tried not to watch as she crossed her legs and her skirt rode up just a little higher on her thigh. It didn't matter, his body reacted simply to her nearness. She could be dressed like an Eskimo and he'd still get a hard-on.

Turning on the power and pressing the appropriate buttons, James waited while the song loaded. He'd finished recording it last night and hadn't been able to wait until she heard it. Now, as it turned out, was the perfect time.

The music started, soft and slow and he looked at Serena until her gaze met his. "I wrote this song about two years after I'd left Baltimore."

It was a ballad, Serena thought, the keyboard playing a solitary tune that held a heartbreaking melody. When James began to speak, his deep voice overlaying the music cast a dreamy spell over the entire room.

"It was one night while I was in my apartment alone. I'd had a really rough day trying to convince this group to let me be their lead singer. I had never felt so alone in my life."

The music continued to play but her attention was focused on the man. Their gazes held as if they were communicating on some telepathic level.

"It was then that I realized," he took a deep breath, "how much I missed you."

Serena's breath caught just as the first lyrics began.

How can I say I'm sorry for all the hurt I've caused?
How can I take away the pain?

How can I tell you that you meant the world to me?
How can it be that we ever fell apart?

It was James. It was his voice singing with the music on
that track. He stood there across the room looking at her
as if he wanted to say these words himself, but instead he
allowed the song to do the talking for him. Serena blinked
back tears and continued to listen.

You were my friend, my lover, my everything.
You gave your heart and soul and I let it slip away.
There's no excuse for what I've done and if there was,
I wouldn't expect you to understand.

But tonight, girl, I'm making you a promise.
A promise that comes from deep inside my heart.
I love you more than any words could ever say.
And I promise, I promise, to make you mine.

She would not cry. Serena vowed she would not let him
see her cry. Instead, she bit her bottom lip and waited until
the song had ended, waited until his words no longer ripped
through her soul. Then she took a deep breath and un-
crossed her legs. It was hot in here, too hot and too confined
for her to stay. She attempted to get up but he was kneeling
in front of her before she could make another move.

"Let me make it up to you, baby girl," he whispered. His
gaze held hers captive as his hands found her knees, pushing them apart. "I am so sorry for leaving you when I
should have taken you with me."

Oh, no. The words she'd wanted to hear for so long
were about to become a reality, but Serena couldn't take
it. "No." She shook her head wildly. "I don't want to hear
this. I don't want to talk about it. It's done."

James pushed her skirt up past her thighs. "I know I hurt you, Rena. Let me make it better."

"No," she whimpered. He couldn't make it better. He couldn't take away all those years, all those lonely nights she'd longed for him. "You can't."

"Yes," he said and bent his head to kiss her inner thigh, "I can. Just relax and let me take care of you."

He spread her legs so that Serena had no other choice but to sit back in the chair. His tongue touched her center in one feather-light stroke. She shivered. He licked her from her hole to her clit in one tortuously slow motion. Her head fell back against the wall and she sighed. "James."

She tried to focus on the physical, to let herself only enjoy the way his tongue was moving along her pussy lips and the way he gently sucked her clit. She did not want anything to intrude on the fantastic physical connection she and James had. Not even the emotional turmoil he'd thrust her into. But it was to no avail.

With each loving stroke of his tongue she felt herself slipping deeper. She wanted him inside her, wanted to feel the deep penetration of his strong cock, pushing into her mercilessly. Then she could block out the emotion building inside, she could resist the feelings that struggled to break free. She wanted him hard and fast and she undulated her hips to send him that message.

Instead, he used one hand planted firmly against her stomach to hold her still while using the other to slip his finger inside her throbbing center. She moaned and he slid that finger along the upper wall of her cunt, slowly until she jerked in response. He'd found her spot. It had never been lost to him. He stroked her there, once, twice, she lost count with the exquisiteness of his touch.

Her body bucked and thrashed on that chair but James did not waver. His tongue busily worked her clit while he finger-fucked her senseless. She moaned low and deep then the sound changed to a high-pitched wail. Her chest heaved as she struggled for breath against the rising wave of pleasure building within her.

His head bobbed between her legs, the sound of her essence against his mouth loud and stimulating. He worked her slowly but persistently, pulling every juice, every moan, from her. She grasped the back of his head, holding him tightly to her pussy, lifting her legs so that the heel of her foot rested on the edge of the chair, giving him even more access. She was coming, her mind roared with the physical release as her body tensed, the world around her going dark but for tiny sparks of light shooting wildly through the air.

James felt the moment her orgasm overtook her and could not hold off another minute. Her sweet taste had driven him wild. The slow pace designed to torture her, to put her under his spell, had backfired. Instead, he wanted her more desperately than he ever had before. Rising above her, he quickly undid his pants, watching as her eyes remained closed, her breasts heaved and she tried to regain her senses.

Letting his gaze slip lower he saw her pussy, shining with her arousal, its scent calling to him. His pants fell to the floor with his boxers, his erection jutting forward. He grasped his dick, stroking it while he looked at her still pulsating pussy. Never before had the sight of a female's genitalia excited him so much. Her lips were plump, her clit hard and distended, her hole seeping with juices that slipped down her crack.

He inhaled the heady scent of her arousal and groaned, then lifted her legs in his arms, positioning himself over her. "Look at me, Rena!" he growled and waited until her eyes opened.

"I'm sorry," he said quietly. "I'm so very sorry." Then he slipped inside of her with a restraint he hadn't known he still possessed. His dick traveling the heated path of her vagina, her walls clasping instinctively around him.

His teeth clenched as he buried himself to the hilt then pulled out slowly. Her eyes glazed as she whispered his name over and over again. He sank into her heat once more, pulled out and fell in again.

Her pussy was slick with juices, yet tight with need. He assuaged that need and felt more of his own growing, expanding. There was so much more he wanted from her, so much more he needed. But this, this connection would always bind them, always keep them in each other's hearts and minds. He'd had no doubt of this. What he did doubt was whether or not Serena would open herself to it again.

She was with him now, there was no doubt about that fact. Her body quivered with each thrust, her center creaming even more when he rubbed against her clit. She was there physically, he only needed to get her there emotionally.

Somewhere, it sounded so far and so distant, Serena still heard the music. The sad but poignant love song James had played for her, had sung for her. Her mind wrapped around the words as it replayed over and over again, as he stroked her over and over again. He was sorry. He loved her. He was making love to her.

It was all too much and she felt the sting of tears escaping. James shifted so that she was now laying on the chair, one leg propped against the back while the other dangled to the floor. His dick was so far inside her she felt as if she would choke on its massiveness. His slow movements picked up and she heard the slap of his testicles against her wet bottom. Her body ached with need and she couldn't resist slipping a hand between them to finger her clit.

"Yes," James growled. "You want to come again, don't you?"

"Oh, yes!" she screamed and moved her finger faster.

James pumped her harder, thrusting his hips until the head of his dick bottomed out inside of her. He watched her touch herself and knew desire hotter and more intense then he'd ever known before. Something about her small hand working the hardened bud while his dick slipped in and out of her pushed him over the edge.

Her legs quivered and he knew she was ready. "Let it out, baby girl. Let it all out."

She yelled and did just as he said. His pumps intensified with that sight until he felt a tingling in his spine and then his own powerful eruption seeping into her core. His entire body tensed, his mind going black as his coming filled her and overflowed, gushing out of her hole, mingling with her juices.

He fell forward, being careful to hold most of his weight off of her. Sweat dripped from his forehead to hers and she giggled. "You're getting me all wet," she sighed.

"Baby girl," he gulped in a chunk of air, "you're already wet enough for the both of us."

CHAPTER SIX

Could this night get any better?

Steven had taken her key and was letting them into her apartment. Cally stared at his broad back, then at his handsome face as he moved to the side to let her enter first. All through dinner she'd thought of what a good catch Steven Bradford actually was. He was going to make some woman very happy one day.

Too bad that woman wouldn't be her.

Turning on the lamp in the living room, Cally heard the door close and saw Steven taking a seat on the couch. She didn't mind that he'd made himself at home. She was actually looking forward to the moment they returned to her apartment. His nearness throughout dinner had her strung so tight she was sure she would explode the moment he touched her.

Moving to the small end table, she picked up the phone to listen to her messages. Steven may not be her man but she still didn't need for him to hear her personal telephone messages. One call from her mother, one from Nola and one from . . . Drake. Cally sighed. Drake had a nice voice too. She must have a weakness for strong male voices because her chest tightened as she listened to him tell her he missed her and couldn't wait to see her. She'd call him when Steven left.

Then she looked over at Steven, at his muscled thighs through his dress slacks and pictured the things she planned to do to him tonight.

Maybe she'd be calling Drake in the morning.

"Something wrong?" Steven asked when she only continued to stare at him.

Cally put the phone onto its base and smiled. "Not a thing," she replied saucily.

He motioned for her to join him on the couch and she happily obliged. "Did you enjoy yourself this evening?" he said, wrapping his arm around her shoulders.

Cally cuddled closer to him, enjoying his strong hold. She inhaled deeply. "Yes, I did. Thank you." Damn, he smelled good. Was there anything about this man that she didn't like?

"How about you?"

Steven kissed her chastely on the forehead. "I'm having a wonderful time. I always thought you were an intriguing woman. I'm glad I'm finally getting the chance to know you."

As he talked her pussy pulsated and she realized she was tired of all this conversation. With smooth agility she straddled him. "Are you ready to get to know me even better?"

Steven's hand instantly went to her hips. "Better than I did the other day?"

Cally undid the tie at her waist that held her top together. The vibrant red material slipped silently to the floor. Her breasts—the size D cups that she was very proud of—jutted forward, almost spilling from her bra. She leaned closer until she could feel Steven's warm breath fanning over them. "Better," she whispered.

His eyes fell to the heaving mounds as she knew they would. His fingers clasped her hips. "You have very nice breasts."

Cally squirmed, trying to get closer to the bulge she felt growing in his pants. "Thank you. Would you like to touch them?"

"No," he growled. "I'd like to devour them."

And that he did. In a quick move his face was buried in her cleavage, his teeth scraping her sensitive skin. Cally gasped at his fierceness, immediately turned on by this shift in his demeanor. In the office he'd had a cool command about touching her. And when he'd tasted her that command had turned to an easy dominance that she had no intention of denying. Now, without his hands touching them, he suckled her breasts, using his teeth to pull down the sheer fabric of her bra until her nipples bounced freely in his face.

He licked one until it puckered hard and long. He closed his teeth over it and tugged. Cally moaned deeply. He repeated the action with her other breast and she slipped her hands between her legs, pushing her skirt up so that she could touch herself.

"Don't," Steven said adamantly and moved her hands to the side.

She looked down to find him staring up at her pointedly.

"I will make you come, when I'm ready."

There was that dominance again. In his serious, no-nonsense way he commanded her and this sexual encounter.

"Let me help you," she offered, her hands moving to unbuckle his belt and his pants. She did not look down but felt his dick spring free against her hand. Wrapping her fingers around his length, she stroked him.

Steven's hands returned to her waist, his mouth to her breasts and he continued to nibble as she fondled him. Cally was so hot she was ready to scream. The sting of his teeth on her nipples followed by the warmth of his tongue sent shivers of ecstasy up and down her spine. She undulated her hips and prayed he would enter her soon.

"You want it, don't you?"

"Yes," she whimpered and ground her center against her hand that still held his swollen sex. If she just moved a little to the left he would slip inside of her. She shifted and felt his tip rubbing against her clit. She clenched her teeth and moved again. The broad head of his erection slid along her moistened folds to touch her entrance. "Oh, yes." She was on fire for him. Thinking about this moment all night had her in a very aroused state that only the good doctor could alleviate.

Without a word Steven stood, keeping hold of her hips as he did. Instinctively, Cally wrapped her legs around him.

"I won't take you on the couch just like I wouldn't take you in the office," he groaned the words over her lips, then plunged his tongue deeply into her mouth.

He kissed her until she was breathless then pulled away and asked, "Which way is your bedroom?"

"Back and to the left," she sighed, tugging on his bottom lip then licking its smoothness. He squeezed her buttocks on the walk to the bedroom and Cally felt a fresh gush of arousal coming from her center. He would probably have a wet spot on the bottom of his shirt when he put her down.

He lay her in the center of her bed and stared down at her. Cally wasn't in the mood for dramatics. She hurriedly pushed her skirt down her legs, tugging her thong along with it. Her bra hung on her in some fashion but she pulled that off too. He was still fully dressed, still standing at the edge of her bed. But for his thick arousal sticking out of his pants she would never guess he was game for what they were about to do. His features were stoic, his stance calm, certain.

"I can undress you too, if you'd like," she said in a voice meant to be alluring but sounded timid.

Steven Bradford did not intimidate her. She'd had plenty of men in her bed, in her living room, wherever. She was no shy schoolgirl when it came to sex. So why was she sitting in the middle of her bed waiting for him to make the next move?

"I want to look at you first."

She blinked, looked down at herself, then back up at him. "You've seen me and thousands of other women naked before. What's the fascination?"

Steven walked to the side of the bed and sat down. Looping an arm around her waist, he pulled her to sit next to him. "No two women are alike, Cally." His hands cupped her face. "You have a round face, with high cheekbones and sultry eyes. Your lips are . . ." He leaned forward and stroked his tongue over her mouth. "Quite kissable."

"Tha—"

He put a finger to her lips to stall her words then let his hands slide down to caress her shoulders, her collarbone. "Your skin is so soft and smells so sweet."

With gentle hands he pushed her back on the bed. His gaze fell to her breasts and he cupped each one in his palm. "Your breasts are simply magnificent. Do you know that there are women paying thousands of dollars to get breasts this perfect in size and feel?"

The room suddenly grew very hot. His words could, to anyone else, sound very clinical and unattractive. But to her, in the quiet of her room, in his voice, they were a sweet seduction weaving her into a tight knot of need.

"Your waist isn't tiny like so many women strive for. I can get a good grip on you and not be afraid you will break beneath my touch." He inhaled deeply. "Your hips are lush and inviting. Your thighs, thick and tempting."

He was touching each part of her anatomy that he described. With featherlike gentleness he explored her until her body hummed with awareness. She wanted him so badly she ached. He was so close and yet so far away. She opened her legs slightly and heard his sharp intake of breath.

"Each time you got up on that table and opened yourself I thought I would die of pleasure."

His palm hovered over her juncture and although he didn't touch her the heat was palpable. Then he cupped her, his entire hand holding her throbbing center in a grip that was neither kind nor cruel.

Cally grabbed handfuls of the comforter. "Steven," she whispered.

"I've wanted to hear my name on your lips for so long," he admitted, then slipped one finger into her velvet heat.

"Steven," she said again, this time in a tone that clearly begged him to move further.

He pulled his finger out of her quickly with a slick popping sound, then put it into his mouth. "Mmmm, tasting you was only the beginning."

He stood, spreading her legs wider apart. "Do you hear me, Cally?"

She opened her eyes and saw him standing over her.

"This is only the beginning," he said seriously, then began to unbutton his shirt.

She watched him as he undressed, moving with slow precision that was designed to drive her crazy—which it did. But when he was totally naked she felt fresh waves of heat overtake her. He was toned and beautiful, that bronzed skin shimmering in the dim light of the room. The dark nest of curls at his groin giving way to his long erection. She reached for him and he climbed onto the bed with her.

Using his knees, he pushed her legs further apart and groaned at the sight of her before him. Steven had spent many a night dreaming of her creamy folds opening for him, waiting for him to claim. Her scent, musky and womanly drifted up to his nostrils. He inhaled deeply, knowing he'd never forget it, that he'd never get enough of her.

"Please, Steven. Take me."

Her words cascaded over him, blood rushing furiously through his head to his groin. He was harder than he believed he could ever be, his manhood straining to get inside of her.

Still, he waited.

What he waited for he wasn't quite sure.

Cally wanted him to have sex with her. There had been no doubt about that since Monday morning in his office. And he wanted to have sex with her, what man wouldn't?

Yet he waited.

His dick pulsated and dripped with his excitement as he looked down at her plush body, waiting and willing for him. When she lifted her knees and slipped a finger between her folds he was lost.

He moved her hand away. "I told you I would make you come."

"Then do it. I'm not in the mood to wait forever," she huffed.

Pushed by her tight words and more confused by the thoughts going through his head than he should be, Steven did the only thing he could. He thrust his hot length inside her with smooth precision, sinking inside her heat until his balls rested against her core.

She moaned and he held still. She writhed and he held still. She called his name and he grasped her hips, keeping his body still while planted deeply inside of her.

He pulled out until only the tip remained. She reared up, trying to bring him back inside. He pushed her roughly until she flopped back down onto the pillows. Her eyes went wide with shock as he thrust into her again with enough force to rattle her teeth. She moaned and began playing with her breasts.

He watched her hands kneading the heavy mounds and his mouth watered. He pumped her once, twice, with hard thrusts that made her breasts jiggle in her hands. "Is this what you wanted?" he growled.

"Yes," she panted.

Then that's what he'd give her. He fucked her hard and fast, his body slamming into hers with such ferocity he feared he might actually harm her. Her moaning and pleas for more drove him and he pistoned into her with more force, more pent-up frustration than even he knew he had. He'd wanted her for a very long time. His dreams had consisted of claiming her and of them being together, like this.

She wanted sex and she wanted it for this weekend only.

Therein laid his dilemma.

Pounding into her, hearing her wet pussy take him in and out, feeling her walls clench his dick, drove Steven to the edge. She bounced beneath him, thrusting her hips in time with his movements. She was pinching her nipples now, telling him how close she was, how much she needed this.

Faster and faster he pumped into her pussy, sweat trickling down his back and covering his brow. This is what she wanted so this is what he'd give her.

The moment her thighs began to quake he pulled out of her. She gasped, about to question him when he lifted her and turned her over onto her belly. Hoisting her up on her knees he grabbed a handful of her hair. "You wanted to be fucked, right?"

Cally groaned. "Oh, yes. Fuck me, baby."

His dick, still slick from her juices, slid down her crack. He hovered over her anus, feeling his tip bump against the puckered hole. Everything in him wanted to push inside, to claim her in this most guttural way. But he shifted, sliding down to her juicy pussy and sank inside. She pushed back against him and he growled.

The pace was set, wild and heated as he pumped and she pumped back. She screamed and he moaned. Her pussy opened and his dick slid inside. Her juices flowed around him like a waterfall. He reached down and fingered her clit, letting his fingers marvel in the moist haven. Her body began to shake, her moaning subsiding to a steady hum.

He rammed into her harder and harder knowing she was coming, feeling the gush of fluids against his dick and his balls.

"Steven!"

The sound of his name echoed in his ears and he finally lost himself in her, his own release spewing deep inside, filling her then seeping out to drip onto the bed.

Exhausted both mentally and physically, he wrapped his body over hers and let them both fall to the bed.

She did not speak. Steven took that as a sign that she had gotten what she wanted. He slipped out of her and climbed off the bed, heading toward the bathroom.

For endless moments Cally lay there, in the middle of her bed, her legs still spread, her heart beating frantically.

What the hell was that? her mind screamed.

Remnants of that fantastic orgasm still slithered through her body, causing her to shiver one more time. She'd wanted him and he'd definitely wanted her. They both knew that having sex was inevitable. But this, what had just happened seemed way beyond what Cally normally experienced as having sex.

He'd touched her so gently at first, speaking about her body parts as if he worshiped them in some way. His words had warmed her completely, sparking a deeper need she hadn't yet acknowledged. She'd wanted him inside her so desperately and when he obliged she'd felt full and even more aroused.

But the deep, subtle connection she'd felt between them in the beginning had shifted to something different. Something primal and fierce and electrifying. Her legs quivered again.

And now he was gone. And Cally was at a loss for words.

"I'll have to double up on my appointments tomorrow and find a replacement for the weekend call duty," Steven began, speaking the moment he stepped out of the bathroom.

Cally lifted up and watched as he collected his clothes.

"Will you be ready to leave around six on Friday evening?"

"Ah, yes. Yes, six is fine." She was still a little bewildered by what had transpired between them. The fact that he was hastily getting dressed now only confused her more. "Do you have an appointment to get to now?" She tried to keep her voice light, to conceal the fact that she desperately wanted him to stay.

Steven paused. He sat on the edge of the bed with his pants pulled halfway up and one shoe already on. He turned to look over his shoulder at her. "No. But I have an early morning."

Cally looked over at the clock. "It's barely eleven o'clock," she offered dismally.

He was silent for a moment, then he reached for his other shoe and put it on. "I need to go."

And that was that, she thought. "Okay." Slipping off the bed, she walked past him to behind the door where her robe hung. Slipping the deep cranberry-colored silk on and belting it, she looked at him. "I'll pick you up at six-thirty on Friday."

Steven stood and with a tight expression looked down on her. Cally thought he was going to say something. He lifted his hand then stopped before his fingers could touch her cheek. He pulled away and said stiffly, "No. I'll pick you up."

He brushed past her quickly. "Steven," she called his name but he was already out of the room.

"I'll see myself out," he said from the hallway.

Not a minute later she heard her front door open and close.

And he was gone.

"Dream about me tonight," James whispered in her ear as they stood by the door in her apartment.

Serena smiled. How could she not dream about him? They'd shared a magnificently sweet afternoon. From the gentle, yet emotional sex in his studio, to the ride back to his apartment, the shower and then the torturously languid way he'd made love to her again in his bed. Dinner had been impromptu, a large pepperoni pizza and a pitcher of beer. They'd spent the duration of the evening walking through Druid Hill Park like they used to do when they were in college.

Now he was dropping her off at home. He would not stay the night, they'd agreed on that, though a huge part of her wanted him to. So many things had changed today. She'd learned a lot about the man James had become and at the same time had concluded that there was so much more to find out.

But did she really want to?

Did she want to know everything that happened to him in L.A.? She sensed that his return to Baltimore was not so cut-and-dry as he claimed, then accepted that she had no right to ask him about it again. She'd gone into this agreement with no expectations and already he'd exceeded that.

This was not a love affair. She and James were not back together and they were not headed for happily-ever-after. Serena knew that because she couldn't afford to let herself believe anything else.

"Today was great. If I still believed in fairy tales I would most definitely dream about it tonight," she said whimsically and settled into his embrace.

James kissed the tip of her nose. "Good, that was my goal."

"Why do you want me to dream about you?" she asked seriously, then sighed. "We've been down this road before, James, and we know where it ends. Let's not color this picture anymore than we have to."

Was that disappointment she saw in his eyes?

"Yes, we've traveled a road similar to this one but we've both changed since then. Our wants and needs are different. We're different, Rena."

She sighed and looked away. With a finger he tilted her chin until she was staring in his eyes once more.

"You need to know that I want more than this weekend.

I'm still in love with you and I'm going to show you we are meant to be together."

Words she wanted to hear seven years ago now echoed in her living room. She did not want to hear them now. She could not. "James," she began.

He kissed her, his tongue slipping effortlessly into her mouth and coaxing hers into a wonderfully slow mating. She didn't try to pull away but wrapped her arms more securely around his neck and moaned. Damn, but she loved kissing him.

"Go to sleep and dream about me, baby girl," he said quietly then turned to leave.

Serena closed and locked the door behind him, then leaned against it and groaned. "Dammit!"

"It's a battle of wills and I'm determined to be the winner," Nola said as she leaned back against her headboard.

"I can't wait to meet the man who has engaged Nola in a sexual duel," Cally giggled.

"You and me both," Serena added.

They were on a three-way call on Wednesday night . . . well, Thursday morning, since it was long after midnight.

"Anybody heard from Jenna again?" Serena asked.

"No, but like I told Nola earlier, my mother said she didn't look too well when she saw her yesterday."

Nola sighed. "It's probably just morning sickness or some other pregnancy-related ailment."

"I don't know. I think something more than the pregnancy is bothering her," Cally added.

"Really? Maybe she is having second thoughts. Eddie is an old-assed man compared to Jenna. She's probably scared to death." Serena had finished another beer and feared she would either piss the rest of the night away or have a terrible hangover when she arrived for her appointment at ten tomorrow morning—probably both.

"Well, she's having his baby now so she's stuck with him," Nola added. "I can't believe she wasn't on some kind of birth control."

"Why? Are you?" Serena asked, then kept talking when nobody answered. "Maybe she planned the pregnancy."

"No," Cally said adamantly. "I definitely do not believe she planned to get pregnant. At least not this soon. She seemed haunted, though. Like there was something she wanted to tell us but couldn't quite find the words."

"I know," Serena said, thinking again of James keeping something from her.

"I think both of you are reading too much into this," Nola said, yawning. "She's probably just got cold feet."

Cally still wasn't convinced. "Cold feet that brought her all the way to Baltimore just to talk, I don't think so."

"Yeah, when was the last time she was up here?" Serena asked. "That was a little weird."

"Jenna has always been weird," Nola bristled.

"You're always so understanding, Nola," Serena chuckled. "Hey, I heard you finally secured a date. What took you so long?"

"So I didn't accost my doctor or run across my high school sweetheart. You two happen to be more accepting than I am. I'm not spending time with just any man for the hell of it."

"But he's not just any man," Serena cooed. "He's the law clerk with the lethal tongue."

Cally and Serena laughed.

Alone in her bedroom Nola squeezed her legs tightly together. "Yes, his tongue is definitely lethal," she agreed, laughing along with them.

"So we're all set," Serena said.

"Do you think this will really work?" Cally asked, suddenly unsure of this weekend with Steven.

"All we need to do is take the heat off of us. What they say after Sunday we can handle because we'll be safely back in the city. And with the invention of caller ID we can talk to the mothers when we get ready to. I think it'll be fine," Serena said, although she had her own worries about what was going to happen after Sunday. But those worries didn't pertain to her mother.

"I just want it to be over with," Nola quipped. "Speaking of which, I have to go. I have an early meeting tomorrow."

"With the law clerk?" Cally asked.

"No, not with the law clerk." Then Nola smiled. "That's not until lunchtime."

"My, oh my. You've had him for breakfast and for dinner, now you're having him for lunch. Nola, you better be careful, you might get addicted to the lowly clerk," Serena taunted.

"Oh please, he doesn't have a chance in hell of this thing going beyond Sunday," she said adamantly.

Cally had finally finished the first draft of her article when there was a knock at her door. A quick glance at the clock told her it was just after noon. She didn't groan because mostly everyone who knew her knew not to disturb her until after noon on weekdays.

She stood from her desk and stretched. She'd been planted in that chair since 8:00 this morning, determined to at least get a draft done before she started packing for the weekend. Thinking of her trip brought up memories of last night, of Steven and their intense sex and then his abrupt departure.

She hadn't heard from him since he'd left but then she hadn't really expected to. There was no reason for him to call her today. It's not as if they were really dating. He could very well not talk to her again until he showed up at her place tomorrow night. Strangely enough, Cally hoped that wasn't the case.

So as she walked to the door a small part of her hoped it was Steven on the other side.

"Hey, beautiful. Hope I wasn't disturbing you."

Cally's smile didn't falter, although Drake was the last person she expected to see today. "No, I'm just finishing up. Come on in."

He walked through the door, stopping to kiss her before going inside. Cally closed her eyes and inhaled deeply. She had to get Steven out of her mind and focus on the guy she had in her apartment now. Drake was very good-looking in his gray slacks and gray shirt. He smelled really good too, but then he always did. Drake spared no expense on his clothes and his appearance. This was one thing Cally really liked about him.

"So your article is done?" he asked, taking a seat on the couch.

He looked at her expectantly and she took a seat beside him. "Yes, thank goodness. I'm going away this weekend and I don't want to have to worry about that while I'm gone."

Drake toyed with her hair while rubbing the nape of her neck. "Where are you going?"

"My cousin is getting married so I'm going to St. Michael's for the wedding." Cally hadn't thought anything of what she'd said but when Drake's expression changed she asked, "What's wrong?"

"Why didn't you ask me to go to the wedding with you, Cally?"

Cally swallowed, knowing she was about to go through

this same conversation with him again. How many times could she tell him that they were having an affair only. "First, because you work as much as I do. And second, because I just found out about it earlier this week. And third, because we are not a couple."

Neither were she and Steven but Cally purposely pushed that thought out of her mind.

"We could be so much more."

Cally didn't miss the hint of sadness in Drake's voice but she was sure in what she wanted and she did not want a relationship. "Drake, you knew when you started seeing me that I wasn't the settle-down type of woman. I really don't know why this is so hard for you to accept now. And to tell you the truth, it's starting to put a damper on what dealings we do have with each other." She stood, needing to get away from him for a minute. He was touching her and for some reason it was more bothersome than ever before.

Normally, when Drake touched her she warmed and felt the beginnings of arousal. Today it was different.

Drake came up behind her, snaking an arm around her waist and pulling her back against him. "I want you so much, Cally. Can't you feel it?"

Cally sighed. Yes, she could definitely feel his arousal poking into her back. "You want too much from me, Drake."

His hands moved to her breasts and squeezed. "I'm sorry. I guess I'll just have to settle for whatever you want to give me."

He was thrusting his hips against her backside now, making sure she felt his hardness. She sucked in a breath because he was caressing her breasts the way he always did, the way that usually made her wet. Her head fell back against his chest and she licked her lips, not from arousal but from resignation. Again, she tried to concentrate on the way Drake usually made her feel. In five seconds she could be naked with him buried deep inside her. She could be panting with each thrust while he bottomed out in her. The thought of a powerful orgasm after the rush of finishing an article was surreal and normally she loved it.

But when Cally turned in his arms and tilted her head for his kiss her excitement faded. "Drake," she whispered.

"Yes, baby." He kissed her cheek, her lips, and down her neck. His hands cupped her buttocks roughly until he almost lifted her from the floor.

"I . . . I can't," she said, then looked at him as if she couldn't believe the words had come from her mouth. Never, in the year she'd been sleeping with Drake had she turned down sex with him. Even on the occasions when he'd pissed her off she still slept with him and then she put him out. She had no idea what had changed this time.

"I know you don't want a relationship, Cally. We won't talk about that again," he said and tried to lift her shirt over her head.

Cally kept her arms at her sides. "No. That's not what I mean."

Drake released her shirt but let his hands fall to her hips, pushing his arousal near her center. "What's wrong, Cally?"

"Nothing, Drake. That's my point." She moved out of his grasp. "We had an affair. And it was great while it lasted." She watched as his lustful gaze quickly turned to confusion. "But I think it's time for us to give it a rest. We obviously want different things in life." She stopped there, figuring why keep giving excuses. It was over. Funny how just last night, after dinner with Steven but before they'd had sex, she was still willing to continue seeing Drake. But today, with him here, she knew that wasn't going to happen.

"I said it didn't matter. I won't bring it up again." Drake took a step toward her.

She shook her head negatively. "It does matter. You shouldn't settle for less and I don't want to continue leading you on."

"Cally," he said in an exasperated tone. "We've been together too long for this to end this way."

"Actually, I think we've been together too long, period. I enjoyed the sex and I really do like you. It's just that I'm not capable of anything more. I should have let you go sooner."

He thrust his hands into his pockets. "You weren't keeping me, Cally. I stayed because this is where I wanted to be."

"I know that. But now you should think about being with someone else." A part of her stood to the side and watched this scene, wondering where all the emotion was. Clearly on Drake's part only. Cally didn't feel a sense of loss or remorse. The decision was clear and she was telling him without doubt. What did that say about the type of person she was?

"Is that what you're doing? Thinking about being with someone else?"

Now she was a little shocked at his accusatory tone. "I never asked you if you were with someone else."

"I never was."

"And while we were together, neither was I," she said, knowing that to be true, up until Monday, that is.

"But there is someone else, isn't there?"

Folding her arms over her chest, she glared at him. "I am not looking for a relationship with any man, Drake. Not you and not anyone else."

Drake chuckled and walked toward her. "I know you,

Cally. I know how much you love sex. For you to turn me down means you're getting it from someone else."

She opened her mouth to speak and he silenced her with a finger to her lips. "No. I'm not saying you're looking for a relationship. But I know you have to get your thing off. You're too passionate to sit in this apartment all by yourself without a nice hard one between your legs."

He moved his finger over her lips slowly until they parted, then he attempted to slip it inside, searching for her tongue.

"Who's fucking you now, Cally? He must be good for you to turn me away after all this time."

Cally didn't speak. She wasn't quite sure what to say. Yes, she'd slept with Steven but it wasn't as if she were planning on doing that beyond Sunday. Drake had a point about her loving sex too much to be totally alone. What exactly did she plan to do when Steven was out of her life? And why hadn't she just asked Drake to take her to the wedding in the first place?

"Tell me, Cally. Tell me who's been in my sweet pussy."

She pulled away from him then. It wasn't his pussy, it wasn't anybody's. She was her own woman, not a possession of any man. "There's nothing to tell you, Drake, except that it was nice while it lasted."

Moving to the door, she opened it and waited for him to leave.

With another chuckle, Drake smoothed a hand down his mustache and headed for the door. "You're right. It was nice while it lasted."

He paused in front of her and leaned forward. "You're always welcome in my bed, Cally Thomas. Always." He brushed an open-mouthed kiss over her lips then walked away.

With shaking hands, Cally closed the door and leaned against it. She felt like crap. And not because she'd dumped Drake without batting an eye but because the entire scene, including his open invitation to his bed, left her feeling like nothing better than a whore.

CHAPTER SEVEN

After her early-morning photo shoot Serena had the rest of the day to herself. She decided that she'd use the time to do laundry and begin packing for the weekend. She was in cutoff shorts and a tank top when her doorbell rang. Casting a fleeting glance at her attire she shrugged and went to open the door anyway. Unexpected visitors deserved to see her looking like a tattered farm girl.

The roses that were delivered weren't the biggest surprise, but the card that accompanied them was.

I'm still in love with you. James

Serena's heart immediately began to pound. Last night he'd said he wanted more than just the weekend. The song in the studio said much of the same thing. Still Serena had been clinging to her vow. Reuniting with James was temporary. It could not go anywhere.

This was so because of the way he'd left her before. Serena was bound and determined to protect herself from ever being hurt like that again. Hadn't she limited her dating to two months tops before dismissing them and moving on? Hadn't she made sure to handle her sexual needs via movies, toys, and the eight-week dating method, just so she wouldn't deprive herself physically? She'd done these things purposely so that she would never fall in love again. She'd loved James with all her being for ten years of her life and in one week he threw that all away. She would not give him the upper hand again.

Placing the huge vase in the center of her dining room table, she stared at the beautiful blood-red roses and felt a softness in her heart that she knew was dangerous. Clamping down on the momentary lapse, she immediately went to the phone.

"Hello?"

"Cally? Please say you're not busy. I need you to do something for me," Serena said, raking a hand through her shoulder-length black hair while the other held the cordless phone to her ear.

"Hey, Serena. What's going on?"

"I need to talk. Can you come over?"

Cally, who was still feeling confused over her confrontation with Drake and the fact that it was almost 3:00 and Steven still hadn't called her, could use someone to talk to right about now. "Sure. I'll be there in ten."

"Great. Thanks." Serena let out a deep breath and set the phone back onto the table. She knew she couldn't call Nola at a time like this. Nola would definitely berate her for being so foolish as to fall into James's trap once more. Plopping down heavily onto the couch, Serena thought of how much she loved and depended on both her cousins. While she and Nola seemed to argue more often than not, they were still very close.

Nola was very protective of both Serena and Cally since

she thought of herself as the stronger of the three. And Serena and Cally let her do her thing because they knew why she was so protective. Nola would be very angry if she knew that Serena was having conflicting emotions about James, especially since Nola had been the first to warn her about using James for this weekend.

"You're vulnerable when it comes to him. Why put yourself through that torture?" Nola had said that night they were all on the phone.

And Serena remembered adamantly standing her ground, telling Nola that her feelings were no way in jeopardy where James was concerned because she'd had those emotions under lock and key for so long.

Well, picking her up yesterday and singing that song to her had slipped the key right out of her hand. And sending those flowers had turned the key in the lock. Now Serena was deathly afraid that James Baker was going to unleash those emotions, opening her to his assault once again.

Cally arrived at Serena's apartment in twenty minutes because for some reason traffic was horrendous. She'd come prepared to hear Serena's story, then unload her own dilemma. But when she saw how distressed Serena was she decided that piña coladas were in order.

Serena sat on the couch with her legs tucked beneath her when Cally returned from the kitchen. "Here, drink this. And tell me what's going on." Cally took a seat at the other end of the couch and tasted her own cool drink, letting the mixture of rum and the tang of the coconut warm her belly.

"It's about James."

Cally figured that's what it was. Serena didn't get riled

up about many things but when she did the feelings were overwhelming for her and thus Cally and Nola would come to the rescue. But if this was about James Baker, Serena definitely wasn't going to call Nola first. "What about him?"

Serena nodded toward the table. "He sent me those flowers."

"They're beautiful," Cally said without looking at the bundle of flowers that almost covered the small dinette. She'd spied them when she first came in and she could still smell their sweet scent. It was all a reminder of the wonderful surprise of receiving her own flowers last night.

"And he wrote me a song." Serena traced her finger along the rim of her glass, then took a sip. "He recorded a song and played it for me at his studio. He has a studio in Baltimore because he's planning to stay here and work."

"And how do you feel about that?"

Serena shrugged. "It's his life."

"So was it a nice song?"

Serena stared at the flowers again. "It was a love song."

Cally nodded. This was not good. "He sang you a love song and he sent you flowers. I presume this means he wants you back, for good."

Serena's eyes shot to Cally. "He didn't say for good."

Cally took another drink from her glass. "What did he say?"

Serena sighed. "He said he wanted more than this weekend. And then his card said that he was still in love with me." She put her glass on the end table and fell back onto the couch. "Oh, Cally, what am I going to do? I can't be in love with him again. I just can't."

"Your first problem is that you never stopped loving him," Cally said simply.

"But I didn't want to keep loving him. I didn't want to wait for him. And he didn't ask me to," Serena said vehemently.

"If he would have asked you to wait, would you have?"

"Hell no!"

"Serena." Cally shook her head. This conversation was futile. Serena loved James. Had loved him all her life and that fact was not going to change.

"No, Cally! I would not have waited. How could he ask me to wait here in Baltimore for him while he went gallivanting across the country. He went to L.A., Cally! With all those other women and the flashy lifestyle of the music industry. Why should I have stayed here and waited for him while he was out having fun."

"But you did wait for him, in a sense. You dated other men but you never let any of them get close to you because of James."

"That's not waiting for him. I moved on, sort of."

"You're in denial."

Serena stood. "I am not!"

"Then why are you yelling? Why are you so upset by a song and some roses? For all you know he could do that to every woman he sleeps with." Cally looked down at her lap and pretended to remove lint. "You know you might just be overreacting. I mean, you said yourself that he brought somebody else into your sex life. Does that sound like a man that loves you and wants you all to himself?"

Serena was now pacing the floor. "Sherry was a onetime thing. At least for me she was. He said it was a surprise since we'd talked about it before he left and I'd refused to even try it. But that has nothing to do with this."

"You don't think so?" Cally asked.

"You do?"

Cally sighed. "Look, you know I like James. But I think

he's playing on your emotions. He knows you're still hung up on him and he knows your sexual weaknesses. He's playing on them."

"Being with another woman wasn't a weakness of mine," Serena said thoughtfully. "I never told him that I thought about that."

"You thought about having sex with another woman? You never told *me* that."

Serena waved Cally's words away. "It was just one of those fantasy things, you know, from watching all those movies. But I never told James I really wanted to do it."

Cally needed a much stronger drink than this piña colada but continued to consume the contents in her glass. "So tell me about that whole experience. Was it good?"

Serena stopped pacing. "Was what good?"

Cally rolled her eyes skyward. "Sex with a woman, Serena. Was it good?"

"Oh that. I didn't really have sex with her. I mean, she licked my pussy until it was damn near dry but that was it. James introduced her then escorted her out so fast I didn't have time to ask her any questions."

"Hmm," Cally said thoughtfully. She watched the same movies that Serena did and mostly enjoyed the raw, intense sex but took it for entertainment purposes only. She couldn't say that she'd given thoughts to having sex with a woman although she did have to admit that watching it was very stimulating.

"Anyway, that's not the problem."

"Sorry. What exactly is the problem?"

Serena plopped back down onto the couch. "The problem is he wasn't supposed to want anything beyond this weekend. He was supposed to agree to my terms. That way I would feel that I was in control."

"That way on Sunday you could walk away from him the

same way he walked away from you," Cally amended for her.

"Exactly. But now he's messed that up."

"No. He just changed the course of the game."

Serena stared at her quizzically.

"Look, you told him this weekend only, up front. You told him you just needed a date for the wedding. He asked you for one night in return. You've given him that night. You don't owe him anything else. You can still walk away from him on Sunday."

Serena let Cally's words sink in. She could walk away from James Baker in three days. She could leave him the same way he left her.

"It's simple, Serena. You only slept with him once and that was in return for his weekend favor to you. Then you're even. Don't let the rest of this stuff confuse you. Just brush it off."

"I had sex with him yesterday," Serena said quietly. "On the couch in his studio."

Cally paused her glass inches away from her lips, her eyes going sideways to look at Serena. "On the couch in his studio?"

Serena nodded.

"Before or after the love song."

"During."

Cally put her glass down and sighed. "That's why he sent you the flowers. I'll bet you cuddled and spent the whole night together, didn't you?"

"No." Serena rubbed her eyes. "We had sex, yes. We did cuddle a bit but then we left and went to his place and had sex again," she groaned. "Then we went to dinner and to the park and then we came back here. That's all."

"That's all?" Cally exclaimed. "That's like a date, like he's courting you, Serena. That's why he feels like he can make his move on you because you've allowed him to open the door."

"I'm so confused."

Cally patted her hand. "Don't be. You want to get even with him, right?"

Serena nodded.

"Okay, then don't sleep with him again. Thank him for the flowers but don't comment on the card. Go to St. Michael's and enjoy yourself. Then dump his conniving ass on Sunday," Cally said matter-of-factly.

Serena was quiet. Cally made it sound so simple. "I guess you're right," she conceded because she was tired of talking about it.

"I know. I usually am." Cally smiled.

"Oh, please. Now you sound like Nola."

"Speaking of which, have you talked to her today?"

"No. But I'm curious about her and this law clerk. It's not like her to sink below her standards."

Cally waved a hand. "She has stupid standards anyway. No man is going to be perfect and no man is going to make up for the crappy way her father treated her and her mother."

"Well, you're on a roll with advice today, why don't you try telling her that," Serena chuckled.

Cally laughed with her. "Not on your life. You know how hardheaded Nola is."

"Yeah, I do. So what's up with you and your doctor? You went to dinner last night, right?"

Now it was Cally's turn to be contemplative. "Yes, we had a nice dinner. He's a surprise," she said for lack of a better word.

"How?"

"I mean, I knew he was a doctor and that he was good-looking. And from his little demonstration in the office

on Monday I got the distinct impression that he was a con-
siderate lover. Which, by the way, he definitely is. But his
personality wasn't what I thought it would be."

"Please don't tell me he's an arrogant jerk?" Serena finished off her drink.

"No. Quite the contrary, actually. He's really laid-back
and entertaining. And again, I'll say the sex was off the
chain."

"Really?" Serena smiled. "Tell me more."

"He's just so," Cally sighed. "He's thoughtful and he's
gentle and then at the same time he can bring it. Boy, can
he bring it! I thought my entire body was going to explode
with that orgasm." And then he changed, she thought.
Cally still wasn't sure what had happened to make Steven
so distant after the sex but he'd raced out of her apartment in record time, leaving her sated yet thoroughly confused.

"Then you should have a very productive weekend,"
Serena said.

"I guess so." Since Steven had yet to call her today Cally
wasn't so sure about their weekend together. She had the
feeling that Steven was trustworthy, so far as to the extent
that if he gave his word about something he would stick to
it.

"You don't sound very excited about it," Serena noted.

Cally shrugged. "It's a wedding. I'm not overly thrilled
about those anyway. But since I must be there I'll have to
suck up my reservations."

"And what are your reservations, Cally? I mean, you
seem to be good at long-term relationships. You've been
seeing Drake for a while now. As a matter of fact, why didn't
you ask him to go to the wedding instead of the doctor?"

"Because Drake was already starting to want too much.
Asking him to go to the wedding would have seemed like

I was for the idea of a relationship with him. Which I am not."

"But you've been with him for a year, isn't that a relationship?"

Cally adamantly shook her head. "Not in my book. Drake was a sex partner. He was an ear to bounce writing ideas off and he was company on lonely nights. He was never my boyfriend."

Serena nodded. "I see." Then she frowned. "No, I don't. Explain."

"A boyfriend is there for everything, good and bad, ups and down. He's just there. He's supportive and encouraging and honest and trustworthy. He provides sex and companionship without being asked. I called Drake when I wanted sex and he called me when he needed it. We e-mailed each other with writing ideas and dilemmas. So he wasn't a boyfriend."

"Okay, so what is the doctor?"

Sighing, Cally propped her legs up on the coffee table and laid her head back against the chair. "Steven is or was my doctor. I still don't know if I need to find another one yet. We are attracted to each other and we are explosive in bed. But at the end of this week we'll be nothing more than acquaintances."

Serena laughed. "Acquaintances who have great sex. Do you think Steven could be boyfriend material?"

Cally stared at the ceiling. This was the first time she'd thought of Steven in that way. Since she didn't want or need a boyfriend she rarely thought of any man in that context. But since Serena had brought it up, she supposed that he could be a boyfriend if she were in the market for one. "I guess he could be."

"Do you think he wants to be?"

"No." Cally laughed. "Steven is not James and we are

not star-crossed lovers. He's a doctor who obviously enjoys sex. I'm a writer with my own goals and aspirations. Neither one of us is looking for a real commitment."

Serena was thoughtful as she leaned her head on her hand, her elbow propped against the back of the chair. "Did he tell you that?"

Cally turned to her. "No, he didn't tell me that because there was no need to. I didn't ask him what he was looking for. I told him what I needed and he said he would do it. Case closed." Cally stood, now eager to do anything besides sit here and talk about Steven. Especially since she still hadn't heard from him. It was after 4:00 now and that fact was really starting to bother her.

"Okay, case closed," Serena mimicked Cally's response. "So are you seeing him tonight?"

"No," Cally answered quickly. Too quickly. "I have packing to do tonight."

Serena sensed Cally really did not want to talk about Steven anymore so she would refrain, but if she missed her guess, which she rarely did, she would bet that Cally was thinking a little more about Steven then she was letting on. "I have to finish packing too."

"Well, if you're cool with your situation with James, I'm going to take off."

Serena stood and walked toward the door. She watched as Cally picked up her purse and slipped on her sunglasses. Cally was always so stylish. Today she wore black capris, a black silk camisole, and a thick red belt. Her sandals were red and strappy. Her dark braids pulled on top of her head in a loose bun. Serena didn't think she'd ever seen Cally look less than composed. But today, her eyes had a shadow to them and she looked worried.

"That's fine. I'll call you in the morning," Serena said, deciding that Cally was more together than either her or

Nola and so if there were something bothering her she would either work it out or she'd tell them and they'd work it out together. Right now, Cally wasn't saying anything, so Serena could only assume there was nothing going on.

"Will do." Cally gave Serena a quick hug and was out the door. Walking quickly so as not to think of the conversation she'd just had or the questions that conversation had raised in her mind.

The door was not ajar. Nola should have taken that as her cue to leave. But she was a woman of her word. She'd told Mark that she would be here at 12:30 and so she was. His apartment seemed dark even though it was in the middle of a bright sunny day. Her heels were loud on the polished floor. She didn't yell to announce herself because he should have been expecting her.

The moment she crossed the threshold from the short hallway to the living room an arm grabbed her at the waist, pulling her roughly into the bedroom. She probably should have been expecting that. Mark liked to get right to the point.

In contrast to the living room his bedroom was bright. Floor-to-ceiling windows with no curtains and sleek black furniture was all he had on display. On a far wall was a huge entertainment center with enough gadgets and gizmos to look like it came straight from an electronics store. He released his grip on her and she stood in the middle of the floor. After righting herself she looked up into dark, alluring eyes.

"Good afternoon to you too," she quipped.

"I saw you at the office this morning," Mark said.

He walked slowly around her. Nola refused to follow and stood still while he circled her. "That's not strange. We do work in the same office."

"You were coming out of the conference room on the fifth floor."

"I had a deposition."

"I watched you walk away," he said when he was again in front of her.

He'd taken off his tie, his dress shirt unbuttoned to the middle of his chest. He still wore his slacks but had lost the belt and his shoes. The attire sounded like disarray but was actually kind of appealing. "I take it you like looking at my ass."

He was behind her again and Nola thought she heard him chuckle. Then she felt a quick slap to her left butt cheek and yelped.

"I definitely like looking at your ass. That's why I followed you until you were back in your office."

Her butt stung but she refused to rub it. He was playing with her, taunting her for some reason. She suspected it was turning him on and decided to go along with it for the moment. "I'm not sure, but that may classify as stalking."

"I would never stalk you, Nola," Mark said as he stepped closer until she could feel his warm breath on her face.

"I have an hour and a half. You might want to move this little show along."

Mark threw back his head and laughed. "I knew you were the right one."

"The right one for what?" Nola asked.

He slipped her purse from her arm and dropped it to the floor.

She arched a brow at him. "That's a three-hundred-dollar bag."

"This afternoon will be priceless."

He began unbuttoning her blouse. "You know this is really unnecessary. We have a deal and I have no problem upholding it."

Pushing the blouse over her shoulders, his gaze fell to her breasts and he licked his lips. "This is part of the deal."

Sliding the tip of his finger along the hills of her breasts, his gaze bore into her. "I want you naked and on that bed and then I want you to tell me what you need me to do to you."

Nola didn't need this show. She didn't need this slow seduction because from the moment she'd awakened this morning she'd thought of nothing else but being in bed with him again. So, no, she definitely did not need him talking to her in that low, deep seductive voice nor did she need him taking his time to undress her. Her pussy clenched and she swatted his hands away from her breasts and quickly unclasped her bra.

"No," Mark said adamantly. "I don't want it fast." He slipped the bra slowly off her shoulders, thinking to himself how much enjoyment he was going to get from this ninety minutes with her. For months he'd watched her, knowing she was perfect before even approaching her. She was classy and beautiful and intelligent. She was everything he needed and then some.

"I want to savor every moment I have with you, Nola." He unhooked her skirt and let it fall to the floor, then with his palms on her bottom pulled her to him. "I want this moment etched in both our memories forever."

Nola wasn't speechless. No man ever left her speechless. But she was wondering how she should take his words. They could be construed two ways: one, for the steps to seduction she knew he was working toward; or two, for the tricks that all men played. Either-or didn't really matter to her. She was about to get hers and if Mark needed all this romantic talk to get his jollies off, then so be it.

Loving the feel of his strong hands aggressively cupping her buttocks, Nola grabbed his shirt and tugged. Buttons flew across the room and Mark sucked in air through his teeth. "I'm sure you won't forget me for a long, long time," she said, then bent forward to capture his nipple between her teeth. As she bit down she felt his fingers digging into her flesh and wanted to scream with pleasure.

There weren't many men who knew the right balance of pleasure and pain during sex, but Nola got the distinct impression that Mark was one of them.

Flattening her tongue over his taut skin, she licked his pectorals, one and then the other. As if on command he made the muscles jump and she smiled to herself. He was definitely a show-off. Pulling his shirt off the rest of the way she began pushing him toward the bed.

"Take my pants off, Nola," he said in a voice that was just a little strained.

Nola undid his pants and pushed them along with his briefs down his muscled thighs, stooping to remove the garments from his feet. Coming back up slowly, she breathed over his heavy erection. She hesitated momentarily, trying to decide if she wanted this now or later. Mark decided for her.

With both hands he grabbed her head, locking his fingers in the short silky strands of her hair and guided her. "Put it in your mouth."

Because her mouth was actually watering for a taste of him, she acquiesced. With one hand she gripped him at the base of his erection, squeezing and pulling her hand forward. Again she breathed over his length and heard him suck in air then release it very slowly. Extending her tongue, she grazed the tip while continuing to stroke. He grew harder, his hot dick pulsing in her hand. She inhaled, her nostrils filling with his masculine scent. Her tongue stroked his tip again, this time tasting the salty evidence of his arousal.

Her pussy clenched and creamed so she squeezed her legs together tightly. Lifting her other hand, she grasped his sac, moving the twin balls between her fingers. He groaned and pulled her hair until she thought she felt a few strands break free.

"I said . . . put it in your . . . mouth," he gritted.

Again, she did as she was told, in her own way. She took the head into her mouth, suckling on the bulbous skin, garnering more of his pre-juices. Her hand gripped his length tighter until she knew he couldn't speak no matter how much he wanted to give her another command. She continued stroking him and toying with his balls while suckling the tip of his dick.

Then without warning, Nola moved her hand and took him in completely. Taking a deep breath, she relaxed her throat muscles and let his head slip back further. She held him there a moment until she heard his rapid panting, then she closed her lips around him and sucked. Pulling back, her cheeks hollowed as his length slipped through her lips. If it were possible he swelled even more until her fingers struggled to hold onto him. Taking him in this time stretched her lips but the smooth heat of him against her tongue was becoming addictive. With her fingertips she teased his balls until they seemed to disappear.

He released a sound, something primal and animalistic that urged Nola to move faster. She sucked him fiercely as if she'd been starving and he was prime rib on a buffet. He pumped her mouth, holding her head tightly against his groin.

"That's right, take it all in. Suck my dick like a good girl," he growled.

She grazed her teeth along his length until the tip was positioned on her lips. His hands moved from her hair to her cheeks, framing her face. Nola tilted her head and looked up at him. Their gazes held. In that moment Nola saw his lust, his complete and utter desire for her and everything he was doing to her. His jaw was tight, his lips parted slightly so that his deep breaths could be released. He was handsome as he walked through the office. Right now, with his dick in her mouth, he was exquisite.

"Open your mouth," he commanded.

She obeyed.

His dick slid inside slowly, deeply, until she thought she might choke. But Nola had been giving head since she was thirteen years old. If she knew nothing else about sex she knew how to suck a man until his eyes rolled back in his head. When her lips closed around his swollen dick, she noticed that Mark was not far from that point.

She sucked him until her cheeks grew tired, until his thighs began to shake and his balls tightened to the point of nonexistence. Then he squeezed her head and she knew it was time. Tilting her head back she grabbed him at the base and stroked until she felt the first pulses against her lips. Her hand was wet with her own saliva, her lips were most likely swollen, her throat was relaxed, and Mark was ready to explode. Three hard strokes, two deep-throated swallows, and he was shooting his hot release into her mouth.

Mark held her head close to his groin, fucking her mouth until every last drop had been sucked from him. For endless moments he held her head and she held him in her mouth. Then she shifted, resting her face against his thigh. Her warm breath so close to his groin had desire soaring through his body again. With a quick motion he lifted her from the floor and placed her on the bed.

Ripping her stockings and panties off, he crawled between her legs, spreading her wide before him. "Such a pretty pussy," he whispered.

Nola smiled. "Pretty enough to eat?"

He glanced up at her and grinned. "Most definitely."

Nola's thighs shook with expectation but Mark only looked at her. For a moment she thought he was rethinking what he was about to do. Then he exhaled and his warm breath covered her dripping wet core. He ducked his head and sucked hard on her clit. Nola screamed and he pulled back, blowing on the tightened bud. "Relax, I'm going to take good care of this pussy."

And with that he began slurping and sucking her nether lips, her hole, and her clit. His tongue left no spot unattended and while his tongue mastered her, he was rubbing the bristly hairs of his goatee against her moistness. The contrast was mind-blowing and Nola gyrated against his face in response.

Nola let her head fall back on the pillows as Mark's fingers dug into her thighs and he sucked her faster and harder. Upon her arrival, Nola had been concerned with the time. At this moment she had no idea if it were night or day, her thoughts centering solely around Mark and his magnificent mouth. Seconds later she screamed her release and Mark moaned as he lapped at her juices.

As she lay with the last trembles of pleasure snaking through her legs, Mark pulled away. "I'm ready for you now."

Nola's eyes opened slowly and she saw him kneeling between her spread legs stroking his big, fat dick. "Are you ready for me, Nola?"

Nola did not hesitate. "Yes."

"Then get on your knees and show me that ass." As she moved James reached into the nightstand to retrieve a condom. He watched her spread herself for him and groaned as he slipped the latex down his throbbing length.

If it were possible, Nola's legs shook and another gush

of juices seeped from her pussy. She moved her languid muscles as fast as she could to get in the position he'd requested. Almost instantly, Mark's strong hands separated her butt cheeks and she once again felt his tongue on her hot pussy. Then he replaced his tongue with his fingers, plunging them deeply into her center, then slipping past her perineum to her anus. Again and again he pulled juices from her center to moisten her rear.

Nola moaned and pressed back against his movements, so hot she would most likely set the sheets ablaze at any moment. When she felt his tip resting against her anus she could do nothing but close her eyes with expectancy. Pain or pleasure. Pleasure or pain. Her mind could not distinguish at this point.

And so as he pushed the fat head of his dick into her ass, her fingers clenched in the sheets but her pussy pulsated, creaming once again.

With just the head inside, Mark rotated his hips and closed his eyes. If he kept his eyes closed this scene would all make sense. Entering her this way was what he needed. The tightness around his dick blocking all other thoughts, all other feelings. He'd waited for this for a long time, waited for this possession, this complete dominance over Nola. Adrenaline soared through his veins and he slammed into her.

She screamed and his body shook with erotic pleasure. He held still for a minute, not wishing to cause permanent damage. Her body was rigid beneath him and then she sighed.

"More," was her guttural reply.

His fingers dug into her skin as he pulled out of her, then slipped back into that blessed tightness again and again.

He would give her more. There was no question about that.

She was Nola and he'd waited months for this moment with her.

He moaned as her butt cheeks slapped against his groin; he would give her everything she wanted because right now, it was exactly what he needed.

CHAPTER EIGHT

He was riding her, his dick deeply embedded in her soaking wet pussy. Her legs were propped up on his shoulders, her breasts jiggling as he pumped. The sound of their joined arousal echoed throughout the room and she bit down on her bottom lip to keep from screaming out.

"You are soooo good to me, baby," she heard herself murmuring. "Soooo, damn good."

"Tell me this is my pussy!" he demanded.

"Yes!" she screamed.

"Tell me it belongs to only me! Say it!" He'd grabbed her ankles and spread her legs into a wide *V*.

"It's yours, baby. It's all yours," she whimpered, unable to control the spasms moving quickly through her body.

"Don't you ever forget it. Don't you ever forget who you belong to," he growled and pumped her mercilessly.

She came with a burst of fluids leaking past his dick onto the bed. In her pleasure-filled haze she felt him moving closer to her face. Her eyes fluttered and she tried to focus on his face.

"Jenna. My sweet, perfect, Jenna," he whispered.

She opened her mouth to answer him but then realized that something was dreadfully wrong. Her eyes flew open and she looked into his eyes. "No," she said slowly.

"Yes, Jenna. Yes, you are mine. Now and forever."

"No." Jenna began shaking her head fiercely against his words. This wasn't right. It shouldn't be him. He was all wrong.

He grabbed her wrists, pulling both her arms above her head and holding them there. "You said you belonged to me. You said it was all mine," he rasped through gritted teeth.

"No. Not anymore. Please, I've already told you this."

"You are mine!" he yelled. His eyes were bulging, his lips spread into a thin line. He bent over and took her right breast into his mouth, biting down hard on the puckered nipple. "I love you and only you. You have to be mine," he said in a voice that sounded more tortured than angry.

Jenna screamed. "No!"

He looked up at her, then back down to her breast and licked the spot he'd just bitten. "I will never let you go, Jenna. Never."

"No. No. No," Jenna screamed and screamed until she was sitting upright in the center of her bed, sweat dripping from her forehead, pain searing through her right breast.

"I know we're not leaving until later but I took the day off." Steven walked past her into her apartment because he'd been standing in the hallway for more than five minutes since she'd answered the door and he presumed she had no intention of inviting him in.

"I'm not sure how that concerns me," Cally said smartly.

He turned to face her and said simply, "Spend the day with me."

Steven knew she was angry and more than a little confused but that was just fine with him. He was confused too, or at least he had been that night he'd left her apartment. Here was this beautiful, smart, and vivacious woman determined to sell herself short with meaningless sexual relationships, and for what? He still didn't know but now suspected that Cally didn't know either.

He'd thought about this thoroughly yesterday, the twenty-four-hour time period in which he had refused to call or go see her. He'd needed that time to get his thoughts together, to figure out exactly how he was going to go about getting what he wanted. He was going to show Cally that some relationships did work, that she could get emotionally involved with one man and not succumb to a broken heart or a betrayed spirit or whatever fear she had. And they were going to start with breakfast.

"I like IHOP but we can go wherever you want since I picked the dinner restaurant," he said, ignoring the look of impatience on her face. "I'll wait while you get ready."

"I'm not getting ready." She slammed the door then walked past him to sit on the couch.

Dutifully, Steven followed her to the couch and took a seat. "Okay. Do you plan on cooking, because I'm starved?"

"I'm not cooking a damn thing for you," she said huffily.

Steven reached out and lifted one of her braids, twisting it around his fingers. "I like French toast and bacon for breakfast," he said with a smile.

She tossed him a heated glare. "Then I guess you'd better go find it elsewhere."

"I missed you, Cally."

She rolled her eyes. "I can't tell."

Steven scooted closer to her and kissed her cheek. "I thought about you all day." He kissed her earlobe. "And I dreamed about you last night."

Cally didn't move. "Usually when you're thinking about somebody you call them."

"Hearing your voice wasn't going to be enough." He kissed her neck.

"You could have come over," she said, her voice admittedly softer than it had been before.

"I had a lot of patients and then I was tired by the time I got home." His tongue traced the line of her jaw, pausing when he got to her lips. "But I'm here now."

"So?" Cally knew she was being juvenile but her feelings were hurt. The fact that they shouldn't have been was what had her most angry. There should be no feelings where Steven was concerned. Before this week she'd only thought of him once a year when it was time for her exam. Since Monday she'd thought of him at least a million times.

"So, stop being stubborn and go get dressed. We can have breakfast then catch an early movie."

"I don't want to go to a movie. Since you've taken the day off, why not just hit the road early?"

One hand rested on her knee while he put an arm around her shoulder. "Because I want to be alone with you for as long as I possibly can. If we get on the road now we'll be in St. Michael's before noon and then I'll have to share you with your family."

Was it his words or his mere presence that touched her? Cally wasn't sure but she was certain that dealing with Steven wasn't going to be as easy as she'd projected. She liked him, in a way that she hadn't allowed herself to like another man before. She'd finally conceded that point sometime in the wee hours of the morning. However, she was convinced that she could handle this change in plans. She had no other choice.

"Fine. Let's do breakfast." She was up and in her bedroom before Steven could say another word. She showered and dressed in record time, refusing to put a lot of effort into her appearance because that would mean she was trying to impress him, which she definitely was not.

She was pulling her braids into a ponytail as she walked back into the living room. Her steps halted as she saw him standing near the window in almost the exact same spot that Drake had stood yesterday. Only Steven's stance aroused something in her, something deeper than the physical. He looked serious and sturdy. Cally wasn't sure that using *sturdy* to describe a man was accurate, but that's the feeling she got from him. He looked like the type that when the chips were down he would stick, although that shouldn't matter to her.

"All set?" he asked when he turned to find her staring at him.

She nodded because words weren't readily coming to mind. Retrieving her purse, she mentally admonished herself for these foolish thoughts.

Breakfast had progressed much as their dinner had, to Steven's relief. Cally had relaxed and they'd resumed the easy conversation that seemed so effortless between them. And all through the meal he saw more reasons why his plan to win this woman over was for the best. She was so obviously running from something that he had to concentrate on not telling her that.

Cally wasn't the type of woman that would take kindly to a man assessing her life, especially when he wanted to tell her how wrong she'd been about relationships. She purposely did not mention anything beyond their dinner two nights ago. So for the hell of it he decided to bring it up.

"You're a very passionate lover, Cally. I can't help but wonder why you haven't had men begging to marry you."

She visibly gulped down the swallow of coffee she'd taken, then licked her lips before answering. "I'm a lover, not a wife," she said simply.

He shook his head. "You're a beautiful woman with a healthy appetite for sex. Most married men would say that's a rarity."

"Most married men don't know what to do to improve on their wife's sexual appetite."

"Really?" He arched a brow. "So you think that's why most couples married for a long time aren't that sexually active."

Cally shrugged. "I don't know. It just baffles me how you can sleep next to a hot-blooded man and not want to have sex with him."

"Will you sleep next to me this weekend?" Steven asked.

His eyes grew darker and Cally did not mistake the hunger lingering there. She'd been trying her damndest not to go this route with him this morning but it wasn't working. "Yes. I will sleep next to you."

He reached across the table and took her hand, rubbing his thumb over her skin. "And will you want to have sex with me?"

There was no sense in lying, Cally thought and stared at him boldly. "Yes, I will want to have sex with you."

"And if I'm not willing, will you take it?"

She tilted her head, wondering where this line of questioning was leading but not totally disliking it. "I always get what I want, Steven."

He gave her one of those half smiles that had her nipples tingling. "How will you get it from me?"

He wanted some dirty talk, Cally surmised. She was game for that, especially since some of the hottest nights she'd had were results of great phone sex. Besides, they were in a crowded restaurant. Things couldn't get too out of hand there.

Cally licked her lips then spoke in a much lower tone. "I would climb on top of you."

His eyes darkened more and Cally felt warmth spread through her body. "My thighs would lock tightly around your hips, my pussy hovering right above your dick. Then I'd lean forward and let my breasts rub against your bare chest."

His grip on her hand had tightened.

"I'd be so wet that my juices would drip down onto your swollen tip. Then I'd lick your lips, your ears, your jaw, then back to your lips again. Yeah, I'd spend a lot of time on your lips," she said, letting her gaze fall to his mouth.

Steven wet his lips.

"If you were still resistant I'd suck on your tongue until your dick was thrusting upward to meet my hot, wet pussy."

Steven gasped, his gaze falling to her mouth.

"Then I would kiss down your chest, over your nipples and past your tight abs." Cally inhaled deeply. "I would smell your arousal and know without a doubt that you were ready for me. Then I would feel your hard length against my jaw, my mouth, my teeth." Her tongue snaked out and lashed over her top lip and then the bottom one.

Steven cleared his throat, then with his free hand signaled for the waiter. When Cally opened her mouth to speak again he silenced her with a look and quickly paid their check. He grabbed her by the wrist and all but pulled her out of the restaurant.

They'd parked in a garage across the street from the

restaurant, a fact that Steven was silently grateful for. He opened the back passenger-side door and guided her inside.

Cally obliged, not entirely sure where this was leading.

His mind was aflutter with conflict. On the one hand he'd planned to woo her into submission, to charm her enough so that she'd have no choice but want to continue seeing him after this weekend. While on the other hand he wanted to bury himself deep inside of her, to enjoy the passion and reckless abandon she had when she was aroused. Sex could not be all there was between them because then Cally would be right.

He unbuckled his pants because his erection was painfully pressing against his zipper. When he was free he breathed a sigh of relief, then realized that wasn't nearly enough. He looked over at her and grabbed one perfect breast in his hand. She moaned and his dick jutted forward, pre-cum building on the head.

No, sex could not be all there was between them, but it was a damn good start.

"You don't have to make me want it, Cally. I want you every minute of every day," he said through clenched teeth.

A smile spread across Cally's face and she leaned into the hand that kneaded her breast. "For the next three days you can have me every minute of every day, Steven."

That wasn't totally what he wanted to hear, but he'd deal with that later. For now he needed to be inside of her, he needed to feel her warmth surrounding him. "Reach into my back pocket, inside my wallet, and get a condom," he said, keeping his eyes trained on hers.

She did as he asked then ripped the condom package open with her teeth. "Shall I put it on?" she asked coyly.

Steven looked down at his burgeoning erection and grinned. "Do you even have to ask?"

Cally scooted closer to him and smoothed the condom over his rigid dick, feeling her pussy muscles contract as she did.

"You want it?"

She wasn't even about to lie. "Yes," she whispered.

Steven shifted in the seat so that his legs were spread, his dick jutting upward, waiting. "Then take it."

He didn't have to tell her twice.

Cally quickly unbuttoned her pants and slipped them down and off. Her panties were caught with them. She was about to straddle him when he held up a hand to stop her.

"Take off your shirt and your bra. I want to watch your breasts jiggle as you ride."

Because the words seemed a little out of character for Steven, Cally found herself even more aroused. She removed her shirt and her bra, not once giving thought to the fact that they were in a public parking garage and anyone could walk by his car at any moment. With her hands on his shoulders, she straddled him, making sure her breasts were perfectly aligned with his face.

"You have great breasts," Steven said, breathing his warm breath over her nipples. "Did I ever tell you that?"

"Yes," Cally whispered, wanting desperately for him to take one of them into his mouth. She thrust them forward, hoping he would take the hint.

But Steven just rubbed them over his face, felt her tight nipples against his cheek and then over his lips. The plump globes moved with his ministrations and he struggled to keep from grabbing them and stuffing them both into his mouth. Being careful was an exercise in restraint.

Cally moved over him, brushing her already wet cunt over his hot dick. "If they're so great why don't you touch them?" She pushed her breasts further in his face. "Taste them, Steven."

He buried his face between both mounds and inhaled deeply. She smelled of something floral and something primal. He extended his tongue and licked the smooth skin once, then twice. Her breath hitched and she arched her back, throwing her head to the side. Flexing his fingers, he finally grabbed each mound then groaned as he took one fat nipple into his mouth.

Cally hissed and he bit down on the dark nipple. She moaned long and deep and he sucked the entire nipple into his mouth while fiercely kneading the other breast. She bucked wildly against him and he continued rotating between each nipple, rotating between biting and licking. She was screaming and thrashing when he guided himself into her then she paused, her eyes fixing on him in a hazy glaze.

"I thought I was supposed to take what I wanted?" she questioned.

"I couldn't wait," he said, simply, then grasped her hips and brought her down hard, pushing his dick all the way into her core.

Cally ground her hips above him, settling his long length inside her warmth. Slowly, purposefully, she began a slow rhythm. Up and down, around and back. Up and down, around and back.

Steven let his head fall back on the seat and she picked up her pace ever so slightly. His fingers were biting into the skin of her hips as he guided the depth of his thrusts. Cally loved him completely inside of her just as she loved when he pulled out until only the head was submerged. It didn't matter, it was Steven and his dick was all she could think about at the moment.

Steven, on the other hand, felt himself falling. There was a huge lighted pit at the end of a winding road. A road he'd seemingly traveled for most of his life. And now he was close to the pit, close to the drop-off where he would either sink or swim. With each thrust inside of Cally he grew closer, found himself wanting with more clarity to take that jump.

Opening his eyes, he saw her breasts moving, the heavy globes circling then dropping to the side. They were big and soft and tasty and he wanted them in his mouth again. Obliging himself, he suckled on each breast while she continued to ride him. But when he felt his release building, Steven realized that this would not be enough. He needed to claim Cally completely. If it meant claiming her sexually first, then that's just what he would do.

He stilled her movements, then lifted her off of him, silencing her protests again with a look. Opening the car door, he stepped out then reached inside and positioned her on her back. Pushing her legs apart until one rested on the back of the front seat and the other was planted firmly in the back window, he smiled down at her open pussy.

With a finger he stroked from the hood of her clit down to the base of her anus. She squirmed and he watched as juices slipped from her core, coating her plump nether lips. He inhaled deeply, loving the scent of her, then had to stroke his dick that was straining against the latex to get inside of her.

Cally saw him looking at her, studying her and felt warmth rush throughout her body. She'd been in this position before with him but never had she felt this open and exposed. Her pussy throbbed, wanting him desperately to enter her again. But her mind was reveling in the complete way he perused her offerings. Without a word from him she slipped a hand between her legs and began fingering her hole. In and out, juices began to coat her finger, the slippery tightness causing her hips to rotate involuntarily.

"Yes," Steven whispered and took a step closer.

She moved her fingers up to toy with her clit and watched as he licked his tongue to stroke his lips and pumped his big dick harder. Fire built in the pit of her stomach and Cally found herself deep into the act of masturbating in front of him. Swirling her fingers throughout her pussy, she begged for release. "Please, I need to come. Oh, please."

Steven heard her cry and pushed her hand to the side, sinking his dick into her with one swift motion. From that moment on he pounded her pussy, making her gasp and scream his name. Her scent filled his nostrils, her voice filled his head and he resigned himself to the fact that he was simply filled with Cally Thomas.

Cally panted as his fierce strokes stoked the already building fire within her. She grasped the seats and heard herself calling his name, needing to hear him answer, to know that he was the one bringing her this phenomenal pleasure.

"Say my name again. Say it like you mean for me to take this pussy!" Steven yelled.

"Steven!" she screamed repeatedly, knowing that no other man would ever bring her to such complete submission again.

When his thumb covered her clit and matched the motions of his dick inside of her, Cally completely lost it, letting her orgasm take her in body-racking waves of pleasure. Through the haze she looked up at Steven, realized that he'd been truly focused on her pleasure, and wanted to melt. Orgasms had always been like a contest with her and her lovers, seeing who could get their first, whose would last the longest, and who would be ready to try it all again the soonest.

But today, in this car with Steven between her legs, it wasn't like that. He worked her pussy with the express in-

tent of making her come and now that she had, he was
slowing down his pace so that she could fully enjoy it. Feeling indebted and deeply confused by her softening feelings toward this man, Cally reached between them and
grasped his balls, pressing the spot just between them and
his anus.

Steven's eyes grew bigger. "Dammit!" he yelled, with
veins pulsing in his neck.

Cally continued to stroke his spot and undulated her
hips against his now deep-thrusting dick.

"Cally! Dammit!" Steven cried again.

She squeezed his balls then watched as his next curse
died on his lips, his come pulsating into the condom that
was buried deep inside of her.

He collapsed on top of her but quickly adjusted his
weight so that he wasn't crushing her. He couldn't think
of anything beyond this woman and knew without a doubt
that he would have her, by any means necessary.

Cally stroked his back, absently wondering why being in
his arms felt so good, so right. He had begun to slip out of
her and she missed him already so she wrapped her legs
around him, pulling him closer.

"Cally, sweetheart, as much as I'd love to stay buried inside of you, I think we should get up. It just dawned on me
that we are in a very public garage and that if someone
should happen to walk by I'd rather them not see my
naked ass hanging out of the back of my car."

Cally giggled. "Now you think of that."

Nola soaked in the tub for what must have been going
on the second hour. Her water had long since turned cold
so she reached up to the faucet and added more hot,
something she'd done repeatedly in the time she'd been
in the bathroom.

She never did make it back to her office yesterday after-noon. One round with Mark had not been enough for ei-ther of them. They'd fucked like bunnies for hours and hours until finally at around 7:00 Nola couldn't ignore the fact any longer that she hadn't eaten since breakfast. She'd offered to buy dinner. Mark had refused.

She'd suggested they order in. Mark refused.

He appeared almost sulky and Nola assumed it was be-cause they were no longer filling their carnal needs. And while she'd loved the orgasms and Mark's stamina, her hunger was taking precedence. She showered and dressed and suggested dinner one more time. He'd grumbled something as he sat still naked in front of his computer, and she left.

Arriving at her apartment at close to 8:30 with a bag of Burger King food in hand, Nola rethought the events of the day. She couldn't say she regretted it because the sex was amazing. She didn't allow herself the pleasure of a liv-ing, breathing man often, so she tended to savor the mo-ment when she did.

Mark seemed to have the same mentality. There was no cuddling, no sweet endearments afterward, and—her stom-ach growled again—no cares for anything outside of the sex. Nola wasn't angry about that because this was the game she'd been playing all of her adult life, but a tiny part of her screamed for something more.

She'd quickly squashed that part, eaten her food, and went to bed. She had a sleepless night, which was highly unlike her and while she'd awakened with the intention of going to work, an early-morning telephone call from her mother had changed her mind.

"Bill Cole, a professor at the college, was invited to the wedding. You know he taught Jenna," Evelyn started say-ing as soon as Nola said good morning. "Anyway, he's recently divorced but he really wants to be settled down. It's a shame his wife wasn't ready for a commitment. So I was thinking of inviting him to stay at the house for the weekend to enjoy all of the festivities with us. Maybe you could spend some time with him. Lorraine got a little upset because I beat her to the punch but Bill needs somebody on his level. Serena and her makeup job just isn't suitable to his lifestyle."

"Serena's a makeup artist and she's very successful. She's also developing her own line of cosmetics," Nola bristled.

"Oh, I know my niece is successful. You don't have to say it like that, Nola. It's just that I think you and Bill would be a better match."

"I don't agree," Nola said coldly.

"Well, it's not like you're even giving the matter any thought. You're not getting any younger and neither am I. I'd like grandchildren before I'm too old and too senile to enjoy them."

"I don't want kids so I don't see how you're going to get them."

Evelyn gasped. "You never told me you didn't want kids."

"You never asked." Nola sighed. It wasn't her goal to upset her mother but she was in no mood for this conversation. "I just don't see the point in bringing children into this world if you can't promise to love them forever and to never break their hearts. So many children grow up to be serial killers, rapists, or even crazy perverted priests because they weren't loved by their parents. I'm not willing to risk that."

Evelyn was quiet. "He was a fool, Nola. A young, childish fool who didn't know how to handle his responsibilities. You can't base you whole life around his mistakes."

Tears stung Nola's eyes and she quickly blotted them away with the backs of her hands. "I don't give him the time of day, Mama. I'm just saying that I don't want to be responsible for doing that to someone else. Besides, I already have a date for the weekend."

Evelyn's spirits perked up considerably. "You do? Who is he?"

"He's just a man that works at the firm. We've ah . . . been out a few times and I asked him to come with me this weekend and he said yes."

"Oh, baby. That's great. I'm glad you're at least giving some man a chance."

Nola could tell her that this was simply for the weekend. She could say that she wasn't giving Mark a chance to do anything but fuck her senseless, but this was her mother. "I'm trying, Mama," was all she could manage.

After that emotional roller coaster caused by her mother's mention of children and her undoubted reference to the father she never knew, Nola hadn't felt like being bothered with people. And she definitely hadn't felt like seeing Mark just yet.

While taking a bath, she allowed herself to really think about what she'd gotten herself into with him. He was a law clerk and technically beneath her professionally, yet he seemed to be right on her level in the bedroom—to the point that things he did to her were almost straight out of her private fantasies.

She didn't know much about him outside of his name because he never talked about himself. Come to think of it, she and Mark didn't do a lot of talking at all. But this was a means to an end.

A pleasurable one, at that.

Nola couldn't remember the last time she'd ever received this type of satisfaction from a man before, or from herself, for that matter. Her body tingled with the memory.

It was almost noon by the time she stepped out of the tub. She still needed to pack and Mark was picking her up at 5:00. She was toweling off when she heard her cell phone ringing from the other room. She raced to the phone with the thought that it might be the office calling. Picking it up and putting it to her ear she answered, "Hello?"

"You're secretary said you weren't coming in today. What's the matter, you still recovering from yesterday?"

He sounded arrogant and self-satisfied. Still, her body warmed instantly at the sound of his voice. "Hello, Mark. Is this normally how you start a telephone conversation?"

"Only when I'm calling you." He chuckled. "What are you doing at home?"

"I'm just getting out of the tub," she said, rubbing a hand up her bare thigh, needing the contact desperately.

"Mmm, why didn't you call me? I would have gladly joined you."

"I'm sure you would have. Just as I'm sure you had some work to do. Doesn't Leiland have a big case coming up?"

Mark was quiet for a few seconds. "Yes. But Leiland is the attorney, not me."

"You're the law clerk, it's your job to do research and help with drafting documents. I'm sure Leiland utilizes your services." She was sitting on the arm of her couch with one leg propped up on the cushions. The hand that was rubbing over her thigh moved closer to her crotch. The more he talked the more she wanted him inside of her. That was the weirdest thing. Cally was the one with the voice fetish, not her. Although now she could definitely see how arousing it could be.

"My job has nothing to do with this phone call," he said in a tone that was a little stronger than before.

Nola arched a brow, wondering if she'd touched a nerve. Shrugging, she said, "At any rate, I'm sure there is something you could be doing at the office besides calling me."

He let out a deep breath. "What if I said I missed you?"

Nola chuckled. "I'd say you were lying."

"I do miss that way you say my name," he said in a low voice.

"Anybody in the office can call your name." Her fingers slipped between her still-wet-from-the-bath folds.

"But it wouldn't have the same effect. I miss the feel of my dick in your mouth."

Nola sucked in a breath and plunged her finger deep into her center. "Your hand can do the job just the same."

"No. Not the same," he said. "What are you doing now?"

Nola moaned. "I'm touching myself. What did you think I'd be doing?"

He chuckled. "I hoped that's what you'd be doing. Open your legs wide so I can see."

Nola slid down onto the leather couch and spread her legs. "What do you see?"

"I see that pretty-ass pussy all wet and swollen just waiting for me to come inside."

"Hmm, I almost think you have a camera in here." She stroked her plump lips, rubbing her finger briskly in between the crevice, feeling the slickness against her hand.

Mark laughed again. "I have a very active imagination. For instance, if I close my eyes I can smell your scent, I can taste your essence."

If it were possible, Nola creamed even more. She moaned because words escaped her.

"Can you feel my dick inside of you? Can you taste my come in your mouth? Tell me, Nola, can you imagine me there?"

"Oooh yes. I can more than imagine it. I can feel it. You're stroking me just right, hitting my walls and juicing my pussy. You pull out of me and slip your wet dick into my mouth. I can taste my essence on you and I like it. You're pumping my mouth like you did my pussy and I'm sucking you hard." She was panting now, her fingers moving quickly over her clit, her release coming in short waves, a preamble for the big attack.

"Your mouth is hot just like your pussy. You're taking me completely inside. I'm hitting your throat and you still take more. I want to come. I want to pump my hot seed into your mouth and watch you swallow." Mark groaned.

Nola lifted her knees and plunged three fingers into her hole, thrashing against her own hand, needing this release like a drug addict needed a fix. "I'm ready when you are," she said.

"I'm ready," Mark said and they both moaned their release into the phone.

Nola disconnected the call without another word. Just a few minutes ago she'd been thinking that this thing between her and Mark was beyond abnormal. Now, sated and relaxed, she knew that was certainly true, but didn't really give a damn.

Mark hung up the phone with one hand while still grasping his hard dick with the other. He'd come all over his pants and his desk but he didn't care. It was worth it.

In a few short hours he'd pick Nola up and most likely do all the things they'd talked about over the phone. Reaching for a tissue, he attempted to clean up his mess, thinking of how good Nola's mouth actually felt on him.

For the first time in his life he knew that he was truly in love. This woman was driving him wild, making him do things he'd never thought he'd do. He wanted her so badly there were no longer any limits. Everything he did from this moment on was with one purpose in mind: getting his woman.

This weekend was about more than a wedding. It was about defining the person he was, proving a point and moving forward with his future—a future that now undoubtedly looked much brighter.

CHAPTER NINE

"You never told me if you liked the song or not," James said when they were driving down the highway.

Serena shifted in her seat. She'd been a nervous wreck all night and most of the day knowing that she'd be seeing James soon and that their weekend together would be starting. When she'd called him back on Monday she'd been excited about being with him again, about rekindling some of the magic they'd shared years ago—magic that she hadn't experienced with anyone else.

All night long she'd thought of the flowers and the card and that song and she'd wondered if she could really go through with it. But then she'd spoken to her mother this morning. Lorraine went on and on about the activities planned for the weekend, the catering, the bridesmaids' dresses and anything else she could think of that had to do with Jenna's wedding. Serena was supremely thankful that she was not one of the dreaded bridesmaids. The dresses sounded hideous and all the duties required would have clearly driven her insane. Being a guest at this wedding was going to be taxing enough.

The phone call had forced her to focus more on James and the reason she needed him so desperately this weekend. It wasn't just that her mother wanted her to get married. It was because her father expected it. Her entire family expected it. Since she was a teenager that had been drilled into her head, get a job, get married, have a family. That's what life meant to her relatives.

And for a while, that's what it had meant to her.

Then James had broken her heart and all those dreams of happily-ever-after were shattered.

"Rena? You all right?" James took a hand off the steering wheel to gently nudge her shoulder. She'd been really quiet since he picked her up. He'd called her last night but she hadn't answered the phone. He figured she was working and thinking about what he'd said on the card. For a moment when he'd purchased the flowers he'd thought of signing it with something simple, something noncommittal, but then his heart directed the words— just as they had in his song.

"Um . . . yeah . . . sorry, I'm just enjoying the scenery," she said.

James smiled. "You always did daydream during long rides."

"You remember a lot about what I used to do, don't you?"

"I remember everything about you," he said quietly. "Sometimes when I'd be alone in my room at night I'd think of all the fun we used to have. I'd think of the days spent swimming in the creek when you would pack those great picnic lunches."

"You thought about me while you were in L.A.?" she asked, not sure she really believed him.

"I never stopped thinking about you, Rena. You were an important part of my life."

"So important that you left me high and dry." Serena hadn't wanted to discuss his leaving again, especially not with him. But if he was going to come back into her life and tell her he still loved her then she deserved some explanation for how that love could have driven him away.

James's hands tightened on the steering wheel as he smoothly switched lanes. He wished getting through this conversation with Rena was going to go as well. He'd known she had questions and unresolved feelings about him leaving, but he'd hoped they would skip over that part. His mother and sister had warned him that Rena wasn't likely going to ignore their past and pick up with a future with him. He should have listened to them.

"It wasn't like that, Rena."

"Then tell me what it was like." She turned in her seat to face him.

He took a deep breath. "I'd been thinking about my future, about what I wanted to do with my life after college. I didn't want some desk job that my professors swore I would be good at and I definitely didn't want to follow my mother's footsteps and teach. I wanted to see different things and meet different people. I wanted to sing."

Serena remained quiet because she remembered the struggle he went through trying to figure out what he should do. Serena's career goals had always been clear. She wanted to go into marketing and then to open her own business. She just hadn't been sure what that business would be. Helping out with a fashion show at the church had changed her life. Not only did she help dress the models, she'd been drafted by her aunt to do their makeup since she'd been forever sampling different products on her own face. From that point on she'd known exactly what she was going to do.

"Of course I could sing here, a lot of singers come out of Baltimore. But I didn't have the patience to sit back and wait to be discovered. When a talent scout saw me that night in the club and said I had potential that was all I needed to hear. The decision to go to L.A. was made for me."

"And the decision to leave me behind was just as easy?"

"No," he said quickly. "It wasn't. To tell the truth, Rena, I didn't think about that aspect of moving. I couldn't think about it. If I'd taken at least fifteen minutes to consider that I was leaving you and our love behind I probably wouldn't have gone. So I didn't think about it. I couldn't."

"What we had was that expendable."

Without warning James pulled the car to the side of the road. Turning off the ignition, he shifted in his seat and took her hands in his. "What we had was more than I could handle at the time. My feelings for you were so intense that it scared me. I knew that I loved you, that I needed you desperately. But I also knew that if I didn't take the chance to follow my dream that I would possibly end up hating myself and you. I should have handled the situation differently, I know that now."

"I would have gone with you," Serena said quietly. She'd waited so long for this conversation, for him to answer her questions and now her heart threatened to explode with new feelings. She was confused. Should she still be angry with James for leaving her or should she admire him for venturing out on his own? Should she allow their new, more mature relationship to grow or should she let the past remain in the past?

James was surprised. How many times had he considered sending for her? How many nights had he wished she was there with him? "Believe me when I say I wanted you with me."

He cupped her cheek with his palm. "What I wrote on that card was the absolute truth. I still love you, Rena. I've never stopped loving you. I'm so sorry that I hurt you."

Her insides trembled. He still held one of her hands and he was touching her face. A part of her wanted to simply fall into his arms, to let him hold her and tell her repeatedly that he loved her. But the stronger part held back. "You did hurt me, James. And I've struggled for years to get over that hurt, to get over you. Now you're back in town, back in my life and you're saying all the things I wanted to hear you say eight years ago."

"Rena—"

She lifted a hand to cover his mouth. "No. Don't say anything. It's my turn to talk. I've built a life of my own. My business is doing well and is growing and I intend to dedicate all of my time to making it a success. I will always have a place in my heart for you but this," she moved her hand between them both, "this cannot continue beyond this weekend. I asked you to spend the weekend with me for the purpose of this wedding only. Not on the pretense of us getting back together. What we had is over."

Surprisingly the words came fairly easy. The lump in her throat hadn't been as hard to speak around as she'd anticipated. And she was proud of herself for standing her ground with the one man that had the power to destroy her, again.

Her words hurt, James would not deny. But they were just words. She was speaking out of past hurt. She'd never had the opportunity to tell him how she felt about him leaving. Now, he'd given her that chance. The last eight years would now be behind them, James would see to that.

Leaning over, he brushed a finger lightly over her cheek. His other hand rested on her knee and he simply stared at her. "Let's leave the past in the past," he whispered and moved closer.

"James," she began but his lips on hers stopped her.

"Let's just concentrate on having a great weekend," he said, brushing her lips lightly again then extending his tongue and licking. She was so sweet. No matter how many times his lips were on her, the taste always surprised him.

With infinite slowness he lapped at her lips again and again. He heard her suck in a breath and he captured her bottom lip between his teeth and tugged. Her hands went to his head, clasping him so that he could not move away.

"James," she murmured his name because that's all she could think about at this moment. They'd discussed the past; he'd said let it remain in the past. They were headed to St. Michael's for the weekend, for the wedding. So why were they stopped on the side of the road indulging in this too-intense kiss? Her mind couldn't grasp the logic behind question and answers. Serena stuck out her tongue and tasted his lips the way he'd done hers. His thin mustache tickled her lips as she moved in, thrusting her tongue deeply inside his mouth.

James was determined to move slowly. He brushed his tongue against hers but in a languid motion that had her squirming. He angled his head and pressed the kiss deeper but kept it slow. Everything he felt for her he poured into that kiss. All the lonely nights, all the empty dates with women who meant nothing to him, all the times he'd picked up the phone to call her to beg her to come to L.A. to be with him.

He grasped her shoulders, pulling her closer, hugging

her to his chest. She felt so good there, her warmth mingling with his. Her hands held tightly to his head and he
shuddered.

Serena sighed and opened her mouth wider in anticipation. She wanted him to kiss her harder, to rip her blouse
and bra away from her burning breasts. She needed his
hands to move from her back to between her legs, to the
hot spot that seemed to thrive only on his touch. She
inched closer to him, pressing her breasts against him in
what she thought was a blatant clue. He kept her in the
tortuous embrace and groaned.

Her hands went to his chest as she kneaded his pectorals and fingered his nipples. His teeth nipped her lip
but his tongue continued to move slowly over hers. She let
her hands move further south until she was cupping his
huge arousal. She squeezed the warm bulge then rubbed
its length.

His hands tightened around her but still he did not
take the kiss further. She unzipped his pants and felt the
turgid skin of his dick and began to pull it free.

James moved back quickly, staring at her with heated
brown eyes.

"What? What's wrong?" Serena's breathing was hitched
and she blinked rapidly to try and understand his motives.

James cleared his throat and adjusted his throbbing
arousal. Zipping his pants, he moved over into the driver's
seat. "We should get going, we don't want to get to
St. Michael's too late tonight."

Serena gaped for a few seconds more then slid further
near the passenger door. What had just happened? She'd
told him things between them were over then she'd tried
to suck his tongue down her throat while attempting to
jerk him off. She almost laughed. Things were always un-
predictable for her and James.

*   *   *

Jenna hadn't heard from him since earlier in the week. She shouldn't be so in tune to that fact but his newfound silence frightened her. Never in a million years would she have pegged him for a stalker but his refusal to let go of their affair was proof of that.

In two days she'd be Mrs. Edward Remington. She would have a beautiful house, a luxury car, and a bank account sure to cater to her every whim. She'd be set for life and that had always been her goal. Any and everything else was a pasttime.

"Hey, Jenna! You ready for this weekend?" Cally asked the moment she entered the dining room of Uncle Jeorge, the oldest of the Evans family's house. Uncle Jeorge had inherited the house upon his parents' death. The house remained the centerpiece of their family and the mutual meeting place whenever they had get-togethers. Aunt Lorraine had told her that Jenna was in here cataloging some of the gifts that had arrived by mail this week. Boxes were strewn across Granny Elouise's cherrywood table and Jenna sat at the end with a pen in hand and notepad in front of her.

She wasn't writing anything. In fact, Cally noticed that she looked quite dazed. Not letting that stop her, she went directly to Jenna's side and clasped her in an awkward hug since Jenna still didn't look as if she'd acknowledged Cally's entrance.

"You okay, Jen?" Cally asked, now increasingly more concerned about her cousin. "Are you feeling sick?"

Jenna shook her head as if she were trying to wake up. "No. I'm not sick. I was just thinking about something."

"Whatever it was it must have been deep. You didn't even know I'd come in." Cally looked once more at the gifts on the table. "Do you need some help?" she offered.

"Ah, no," Jenna said absently, but at least looking up at Cally this time. "I'm tired. I think I'm going to leave this for Mama to finish up."

"I can do it for you. Dinner's not for another hour so I've got some time to kill." Cally was about to take a seat when she remembered she wasn't alone. Looking toward the door, she noticed that Steven had already come into the dining room and was pouring a glass of water.

"Jenna, this is my friend, Steven," Cally began.

Steven was walking toward her and Jenna.

"Steven," Cally finished, "this is my cousin, Jenna. The beautiful bride-to-be."

Moving across the room again, Steven stopped in front of Jenna and extended the glass of water. "Hello, Jenna. I'm Dr. Steven Bradford, Cally's . . . ah . . ." He looked up at Cally, at a loss for words, then resumed speaking. "I'm Cally's date. I had planned to congratulate you on your wedding but you look a little pale. Drink this and take a couple of deep breaths."

Cally shouldn't have been shocked at Steven's proclamation of being her date. It wasn't that what he said was false and her goal was to convince her family that she was actively dating. Still, having him say it made her nervous.

"You're a doctor?" Jenna said, taking the glass from Steven with a shaky hand.

"Yes," Steven answered. "I'm a gynecologist."

Jenna had taken a sip of the water and now choked at his words. Cally quickly rubbed her back. "He's a GYN, Jenna. Not an obstetrician."

Steven raised a brow. "Do you need an obstetrician?"

"No," Jenna said quickly. "I don't need anything." She stood abruptly, then extended her hand. "It was a pleasure meeting you, Dr. Bradford. Thanks so much for sharing in this weekend with me and my family."

Steven shook her hand, sure that something strange was going on here. "The pleasure is all mine, Jenna."

"Cally, why don't you show your friend around? I have a couple of things to do before dinner."

Before Cally could answer, Jenna was out of the room. With a frown, she turned to Steven.

"She's pregnant, I take it."

Cally nodded. "She just told me on Tuesday. But I don't think she's told her husband-to-be yet. I'm not real sure why, though."

Steven didn't miss the way Cally's eyes continued to fall back on the festively wrapped wedding gifts. He wondered if she was longing for this day of her own. Of course, he knew she'd never admit to that but there was definitely something wistful about her gaze.

"What makes you think she hasn't told him?" he asked, motioning for her to take a seat.

Cally sat down. "She didn't want you to know she was pregnant. That makes me think she hasn't announced it yet."

Steven took a seat next to her, lifting her hand in his. "Just because she hasn't announced it to the family doesn't mean her fiancé doesn't know."

Cally shook her head. "She hasn't told him and I don't know why. Jenna's acting really strange. I wonder what's going on with her."

"Probably just jitters."

"Why would she have jitters? If she loved him enough to accept his proposal, walking down the aisle should be a piece of cake."

"Would it be for you?" Absently he rubbed his thumb over her hand, keeping his gaze focused on her.

She looked at him and decided to answer honestly. "I've never thought about it."

"You've never thought about getting married?" Steven admitted to being more than a little surprised. Didn't all women fantasize about their wedding day?

"Marriage is not really in my vocabulary." She sighed. "I guess I've had passing thoughts about it but never anything detailed and never anything directed at me. I've always known that I wasn't marriage material."

"Really? Why is that?"

Cally shrugged. "Maybe because I was never good at long-term relationships. I suffer from a short attention span."

"How long did your last relationship last?" Steven asked, because learning more about her was imperative.

Cally wasn't sure why she was talking about this or why Steven had been the one she decided to open up to, yet she realized she had answers to his questions. "It lasted a year but it wasn't a relationship. It was more along the lines of mutual satisfaction."

"If you talked to him, went out with him, and slept with him, it was a relationship," he pointed out.

"I don't think that's true."

"It is. Tell me what you and he did that was not a part of what you believe is a relationship."

Cally thought about that. She and Drake did go out to eat even, if not that often. He called her on a regular basis and she called him the same. And they had great sex. "I don't know," she said lamely.

"You didn't want to marry him, did you?"

"No."

"That doesn't mean you weren't in a relationship with him. And sometimes it doesn't matter how long a relationship lasts to tell if it's serious or not. Didn't you tell me that Jenna has only been seeing her husband for a few months?"

"Yeah, to her parents' dismay."

"They have no need to be dismayed. You know when you love someone. There's no timetable on that emotion. It can happen quickly, overnight. Or it can take its time, years even. At any rate, when you fall in love you'll know it. And your self-induced phobia is unfounded."

Cally wasn't entirely sure but it sounded like he had just insulted her. "I don't have a phobia," she said for lack of a better response. "I have standards that I'm not willing to ignore for the sake of becoming some man's wife and virtual slave."

Steven smiled; now they were getting somewhere. "How does being a wife equate to be a slave?"

Apparently this was a discussion he was determined to have. Cally, on the other hand, had no desire to reenact the scene she'd had with Drake but since Steven wanted to know, she was going to tell him. "When a woman marries she becomes a man's possession. Not necessarily in the slave-master mentality but in that she is bound by her vows to honor and obey him."

"And you would never obey a man? In this day and age there are women who request to have that word removed from their vows. So that's not a valid defense."

He looked as if he were challenging her. He wanted her to give him a good reason why she was against marriage, against falling in love. She had one. She was sure. For years she'd been against marriage and serious relationships; surely she had a reason for it. "Whether or not it's verbalized, it is implied. My mother, for example, married my father forty years ago. She was fresh out of high school planning to make a career in cooking because that's what she loved to do. She could have gone to culinary school or gotten a job in a restaurant to receive the training she needed. But instead she married my father and traveled with him while he was in the service. When they returned to Maryland

she had me. She took care of the house, me, and my father until I graduated high school and my father died of
cancer three years ago. Now she answers the phone at a
dentist's office. Her dream of being a caterer long lost."

Steven had continued to hold her hand as she spoke.
Her voice had been clear and smooth as she talked of
something he suspected was the source of a lot of bitter-
ness on her part. Only the slight tremor of her hand told
him that this admission was an emotional one.

"So you see, I may be one of few, but I am definitely
against the institution of marriage," she said finally, staring at him pointedly.

"I would never ask you to give up your career," Steven
said slowly. "And I'm sure your father didn't ask your
mother to, either. Maybe she chose to travel with her husband and to take care of her family over pursuing a career.
Have you ever asked her?"

Cally shrugged. "No. I love and respect my mother. I
know that whatever she did she thought was the best thing
for her and for her family. I just don't want to be forced to
think along those lines." Cally took a deep, steadying
breath. "Besides, we're here for Jenna's wedding, not to
talk about why I don't want to get married. That's an
open-and-shut book anyway."

"I've always been an avid reader," Steven said seriously,
then stood, using the hand he held of hers to lead her out
of the chair. "But I'll have to entertain myself with that
later. Right now we should probably go to dinner."

Cally stood about to comment on his remark but was
quickly stopped by his lips upon hers. It was a brief touch
that quickly led to a passionate assault as his tongue thrust
into her mouth, claiming this part of her as no man had
ever done before.

*   *   *

Mark didn't want dinner and while it ticked Nola off slightly, she'd closed the door to their room and left him there. He'd pointed out that she'd invited him to the wedding, not exactly to all the family gatherings.

In retrospect she figured that was just fine. Let Cally and Serena endure the question-and-answer session tonight. Entering the huge dining room, she saw that the session had already begun.

Seated at the table was her mother, Aunt Marsha and Uncle Cuba, Aunt Lorraine, Cally, and the man she assumed was Dr. Bradford. With one long glance Nola surveyed her cousin's date and concluded that he was the exact opposite of Cally. He looked serious and stuffy, but she admitted that he was cute as hell.

On the other side of the table was her mother, Uncle Jeorge, Aunt Leola, and Jenna.

"Good evening, everyone," Nola said upon making her entrance.

Her mother instantly stood and went to hug her. During the embrace she whispered, "Where's your date?"

Nola fought back a groan. "He was tired from working all day and then driving. We caught a little bit of traffic on the way down. You'll meet him in the morning."

Cally, who was closest to where Nola and her mother were standing, looked up at Nola with questioning eyes. When Evelyn had finally released Nola, the cousins shared a knowing glance.

"Hey, Jenna. Congratulations again." Nola leaned forward and hugged Jenna. "Where's Edward?"

Jenna's cringe wasn't readily noticeable but Cally caught it, maybe because she'd been wondering the same thing herself.

"He had to work late. He'll be here soon but he's not staying for the weekend."

"He doesn't need to be staying under the same roof with you until you're married anyway. I don't know why your mother has let you spend so many nights at his house," Uncle Jeorge said with mild irritation.

"She's a grown woman, Jeorge," Aunt Leola said quickly.

Nola broke into the argument. "Where's Serena?"

"I'm here," Serena said breezily as she entered the dining room, James right behind her.

Aunt Lorraine hopped up out of her seat, going to embrace her daughter. "My baby. You look so pretty in blue." Then, as if she hadn't noticed the tall man standing behind Serena, she saw him and immediately moved to embrace him as well. "James Baker! When did you come home? It's so wonderful to see you. And to see you two together again."

Serena looked a little panicked and Cally reached out a hand to touch her. "Hi everybody," Serena said when she had regained her composure. "You all remember James, right?"

Aunt Marsha, who was just returning to her seat, smiled. "We remember him very well. You two were glued at the hip during high school. It's no wonder you've found each other again after all these years."

James immediately moved to Serena's side, taking her hand and leading her to an empty seat. "It's good to see all of you again. It feels just like old times," he said once Serena was seated. James smiled and took the empty seat next to her. It did feel good to be back in St. Michael's, back at the hours where he'd spent a lot of time during his teenage years.

"So what brings you back, James?" Aunt Evelyn asked when she'd returned to her seat. "I just talked to your mother last month and she didn't say a word about your return."

"That's because she didn't know. But I've been planning to come home for a while." He looked toward Rena and added, "There was something here more important than what was in L.A."

Serena felt all eyes on her and struggled to keep her composure. Hadn't they just discussed this? She couldn't believe James was even going there with her again and in front of her family, no less. "So what's on the agenda for tomorrow?" she asked, trying desperately to get the focus off of her and what was not happening between her and James.

Nola shook her head with a mixed look of pity and disgust. "Brunch at the Inn and an afternoon at the spa. Woo-hoo!" She made a twirling motion with her hand and rolled her eyes skyward.

"It'll be fun," Evelyn tried to convince her daughter. "All the women will enjoy a great day together and then we'll join up again in the evening at the church."

Nola moaned. "Are all your bridesmaids going as well?"

"Good grief, how many are there?" Serena asked.

Jenna gave a dramatic sigh. "Twenty-two."

"Twenty-two!" Serena and Nola exclaimed simultaneously.

"Are you even old enough to know twenty-two people?" Cally asked incredulously. Why, even if you subscribed to the institution of marriage, would a woman need twenty-two people to stand at the altar with her? Then she did the math and corrected the twenty-two with forty-two, men included. It was insanity. She'd never dreamed of a wedding and she'd certainly never dreamed of more people than it took to comprise a baseball team standing with her.

"I saw your invitation in the living room while I was waiting for Cally. It's nice. Very romantic," Steven interjected.

Cally's head jerked in his direction but she didn't comment. He was acting weird. He had been since they'd first arrived. He seemed to be bonding with her family, a little more than she was comfortable with. Her mother had actually had him carrying in gifts and assisting in the logging process since Jenna had been too tired to do it.

That brought Cally's thoughts back to her cousin. Even after a two-hour nap Jenna still looked tired and worn down. Her eyes were puffy and her usually excellently coiffed hair was out of place. They were eating Caesar salads but Jenna had barely touched hers.

"My mother picked them out," Jenna said quietly then excused herself and left the room.

Dinner proceeded with different strands of conversation assembling. Afterward they were to retire to the back porch for iced tea and sweet potato pie. Nola didn't feel like being outside with the bugs so she stayed inside.

Truth be told, her mind kept reverting back to Mark and his no-show at dinner. He'd said he was tired and that he'd probably come down a little later. That was more than an hour ago and she still hadn't seen him. Once the family was outside she headed up the steps to find him.

Jenna was a nervous wreck. Something was about to happen, she was absolutely sure of it. She hadn't received any more calls or notes, but she knew he hadn't given up that easily.

A quick glance at her watch gave her about thirty minutes until Edward arrived. Edward was very excited about the wedding and very pleased with all the festivities her mother had planned in honor of it. She would just go into the bathroom, splash some water on her face, and pull herself together. Edward could not see her like this. Just last night he'd questioned her about how jittery she seemed.

"Darling, everything will be fine. You will be beautiful. Our wedding will be beautiful and we'll have a wonderful life together."

She'd sighed and rested her head on his shoulder. Edward was so comfortable. He always knew the right thing to say. Entering the bathroom, she sighed at the memory of his voice, his thin hands on his shoulders as he attempted to massage her stress away.

Edward would take care of her always. That's why she loved him and that's why she was marrying him. Nothing else mattered.

She was pushing the door closed when a booted foot jammed it. With a yelp she pulled the door open and almost lost the small amount of Caesar salad she'd been able to force down.

"Hello, sunshine," he crooned in that sultry voice she'd heard in her dreams.

"What the hell are you doing here?" she wanted to yell but didn't want anyone in the house to hear. How had he known where to find her?

"I missed you." He smiled and Jenna felt her insides quiver. His smile always did that to her.

"No. You can't be. I'm getting married on Sunday. You can't do this to me. Not now."

He pushed the door open further, moving Jenna fully into the bathroom before closing and locking it behind him.

Jenna opened her mouth to scream and he covered it with his hand. "I really don't think you're ready to introduce me to your family."

She nodded, a message to him that she would not scream if he removed his hand. He did and she licked her lips.

"That's my girl," he said, grabbing her by the waist and pulling her close.

All thoughts of screaming fled from her mind as he rubbed his thick erection into her. Heat pooled between her legs as she struggled not to give in. "No," she whispered.

"Yes," he said insistently and backed her against the wall.

His lips came down on hers, taking her mouth in a heated assault. His tongue moved deeply into her mouth and Jenna felt her arms lifting to wrap around his neck. It was always like this with him, always intense and hot. And irresistible.

Before she could think another thought he grabbed her butt tightly, lifting her off the floor. She wrapped her legs around his waist and thrust her pussy into his rigid length.

Her skirt rode up her thighs and when he had her firmly against the wall he removed one hand from her butt to slip beneath the rim of her panties, finding her hot and ready.

"I knew you still wanted me," he groaned and sank his finger into her moist depths. "You still need me."

Jenna cried out, only to be silenced by another brutal kiss. He was right, she did still want him. She was afraid she'd always want him. Sex with Edward would never be like this. She'd done everything except write a step-by-step description of what she wanted Edward to do to her and still there'd been no sparks.

Certainly not the sparks that were ripping through her as he stroked her G-spot with that slow, determined precision that he'd mastered. Her thighs shook and she came in his hand. He chuckled and nibbled on her ear.

"Don't marry him, Jenna," he breathed with his finger still circling against her walls. "Please, don't."

"Where are you going and why aren't you outside enduring this torture like the rest of us?" Serena asked Nola, who was on her way up the stairs.

Nola turned and frowned. "If you must know, I'm going to find my so-called date to hopefully get a quickie in while everyone is outside enjoying dessert."

Serena laughed. "You're a freak."

"Me?" Nola faked offense and made her way back down the steps. "I'm not the one who had a threesome."

"Oh please, when are you and Cally going to let that go? I shouldn't have told you." She shouldn't have but she had and now every chance they got it was brought up. Which made her think about it much more than she'd intended.

"When you tell us how it really felt."

They both took a seat on the couch.

"So what's going on?" Serena asked.

"With who?"

"With Jenna. With you. With Cally. Did you see how her doctor keeps looking at her? I think he's really feeling her."

Nola rubbed her temples. "He's cute. I guess she could do worse."

"But she doesn't want to do at all," Serena interjected. "This is just a weekend for her, just like us. She better be careful or he'll be proposing by Sunday."

Nola paused and turned to stare at Serena in question. "What's up with you?"

"Me? I'm fine. What about you and your date?"

Shifting in the chair, Nola eyed her suspiciously. "You

are not fine. You're rambling and you're wringing your hands. Both things you do when you're upset."

"I'm not upset," Serena said forcefully, clapping her hands onto her lap. "I just hate weddings. And I hate the fact that Jenna doesn't act like a woman who wants to get married. And—"

"And," Nola interrupted, "you're in trouble. What is it, Serena?"

Serena sighed and let her head fall back against the back of the couch. "Nothing. I'm just tired."

"You're lying and you're doing a piss-poor job of it. Is it James?"

"No," she answered quickly. Too quickly.

"Liar."

"What's she lying about?" James asked as he entered the room.

Nola eyed James before standing to face him. "What did you do to my cousin? Better yet, why are you back in her life? Wasn't dumping her once enough for you?"

"Nola," Serena admonished.

"No. It's okay." James smiled at Serena, nodding for her to sit back down. "I'll take the first question. I didn't do anything to your cousin. The second, I'm back in her life because I missed her and if I'm not missing my guess, she wants me there. And third, dumping her once was a mistake. One I intend to correct."

Nola was speechless.

"So how's life been treating you, Nola? Where's your date for the weekend?" he asked as he moved past her and took the spot on the couch next to Serena.

Nola narrowed her eyes and turned to face him with a smirk. "Life is treating me just fine and my date is resting. Remember you're only here for the weekend as well," she said with a satisfied smile.

Serena rolled her eyes at both of them because it had always been this way between them. Hot and cold, oil and water, the years away would never change that.

"Correction," James stated and took Serena's hand in his. "I'm here for as long as she wants me."

It was Nola's turn to roll her eyes because Serena sat there like someone had removed her tongue, letting this fool take over her life once again. "Whatever," she said and turned to go upstairs where she'd originally been headed. She'd taken a couple of steps before she realized she had one more thing to say. Pausing, she turned to look at the not-so-happy couple on the couch and then especially to the man. "Hurt her again and I'll kill you."

James nodded and smiled. "Duly noted."

CHAPTER TEN

"**I** have something very special for you tonight," James said when they were alone in the room they were sharing.

It was after midnight and the mothers had gone back to their respective homes until morning. Uncle Jeorge was fast asleep in his section of the big country home. There were three floors in the house, the two higher ones filled with bedrooms. She and Cally always wondered why Uncle Jeorge didn't sell the house or either convert it to a bed-and-breakfast. St. Michael's was a quaint little tourist town that thrived on bed-and-breakfasts; he'd surely make a killing.

She and James were sharing a room on the third floor. Only Cally and Nola were on the floor with them. Whatever they did in this room would be private, Serena had no doubt of that. Still, she felt a little leery about being intimate with him. It wasn't that it was in her uncle's house, because truth be told she'd had sex in his house before. But this weekend, tonight, was different.

"A gift?" she said when he continued to stare at her.

"Something like that."

"You know I don't like surprises."

"You'll like this one. I promise." He kissed her fore-head, then left the room.

Serena lay back on the bed, trying to get a hold of these strange feelings coursing through her. She and James had discussed a lot of things today and he'd given her a lot to think about. But she didn't want a relationship and she damn sure didn't want marriage. This weekend was her idea, it was supposed to be simple.

She stood, taking her robe off, then slipped beneath the covers. She'd showered already and was feeling more tired that she was ready to admit. Actually, she was hoping she could fall asleep before James returned, thus avoiding any more conversation about their feelings or their future. And whatever surprise it was he had for her, he could keep until tomorrow.

Her eyes weren't closed long before she heard the door open and close. She didn't move, praying she could fake him out.

"Hello, Serena," a female voice said.

Her eyes shot open and Serena sat up in the bed.

"Do you remember me?"

Hell yeah, she remembered her. The best pussy licking she'd ever received had come from this tall woman with the long auburn-colored hair. "It was only a couple of days ago, of course I remember you. Sherry, right?"

"That's right," Sherry said with a smile.

Serena looked at James in confusion. "You called her to come all the way down here?"

James, who had been standing near the window watching them both curiously, shook his head. "No. Sherry called me last night and asked about you."

"Why?"

James nodded toward Sherry.

"I've been thinking about you."

Serena knew she had to look like a cartoon character with her mouth gaping open, so she shut it quickly. "At the risk of being repetitive, I have to ask again, why?"

Sherry slipped out of the trench coat she was wearing and moved to the side of the bed where Serena was. Serena didn't miss the black bikini and garter Sherry wore, or the bra that her huge breasts almost spilled out of. Sherry sat down and Serena scooted over to make room. She smelled like vanilla, a heady and very enticing scent. Serena tried to push that thought aside until Sherry lifted her hand in hers.

Serena's heart hammered in her chest. She'd told Cally that being with Sherry was a onetime thing. She had a sneaking suspicion that one time was about to change into two. She looked at James.

"If you want her to leave, just say the word," he assured her.

She looked back at Sherry.

"I don't do this often, Serena. The other day was just a favor I owed James for helping me out of a bad situation a couple of months ago." She rubbed her thumbs over the back of Serena's hand.

Her eyes were gray, almost like a cat. Her bottom lip was full, the top one thin. Serena didn't really know why she was studying this woman like this, she didn't know why her body was warming with her touch, but she didn't say the word for her to leave, either.

"And now you're repaying another favor?" Serena asked in a voice that squeaked.

Sherry shook her head. "Now, I'm acting totally on my own." She reached for the strap on Serena's nightgown and slipped it off her shoulder to bare her right breast. With her eyes trained on Serena's, she brushed a finger over her exposed nipple.

Serena sucked in a breath, then looked to the window where James had been. But James was now sitting on the other side of the bed watching as Sherry rolled her nipple between her thumb and forefinger. He lifted Serena's hand and kissed her fingers, one by one, taking them into his mouth.

Sherry removed Serena's other strap and played with both her breasts. James had begun kissing up Serena's arm and now made lazy circles with his tongue on her shoulder. She closed her eyes to the swarm of heat running through her body. Her crotch pulsated, dripping juices onto her thigh. She opened her mouth to say something, although she didn't know what and Sherry was right there, thrusting her tongue deeply inside Serena's warmth.

Serena didn't hesitate but kissed her back, loving the feel of her warm tongue, the motion of her lips on hers. It hit her then that she was kissing a woman, that she was enjoying kissing a woman and felt terribly aroused. She grabbed the back of Sherry's head, deepening the kiss. She couldn't see but she was sure it was James's hand that palmed her breast. He squeezed roughly, growling, before lowering his head to take her distended nipple into his mouth.

Her body was on fire so when she felt herself being lowered to the bed, the sheets pulled away, her nightgown stripped off, she didn't resist.

"I really liked tasting you, Serena." Sherry smiled and licked her lips, then rubbed her hands over Serena's nipples again. "You've got a great body. I asked James if I could spend one more night with you."

Sherry stopped touching her to remove her own bra. Serena watched as her heavy mounds were freed and her mouth watered. She looked to James and asked, "Is that what I am to you, a favor you can trade off?"

James, who had just removed his shirt, sat beside her again, rubbing a finger along her jaw. "You are everything to me, Serena. I'm trying to make you see that." She opened her mouth to speak and he touched her lips with a finger. "You said you enjoyed Sherry and I know that Sherry enjoyed you. I just want you to be happy."

His words pierced her heart and Serena kissed his finger. "Thank you," she whispered.

Sherry was removing Serena's panties when James kissed her lips. The moment his tongue touched hers she recognized the difference. While she enjoyed Sherry's kiss and was turned on by it, James touched her differently. His kiss was sweet and assuring, yet arousing and addictive. She didn't want to but her feelings swirled around that kiss, centering in a circle of warmth around her heart.

Serena felt her legs being spread and Sherry's fingers parting her swollen folds. James kissed her deeper, rubbing his hands over her breasts. Sherry pushed two, no three, fingers inside of Serena and she gasped.

"You're always so hot," Sherry said then blew her breath over Serena's moist pussy.

James stopped kissing her and looked down at Sherry, so close to Serena's center. His dick hardened to the point of pain. He stood from the bed and quickly took off his pants and underwear, his eyes never leaving the two women on the bed. Sherry was a bronzed contrast to Serena's cocoa complexion, yet the two looked simply artistic together.

He'd never slept with Sherry because she'd been involved with his brother—that's how he'd found out about her special services. He trusted Sherry with his life and now with his woman. She licked Serena once from front to back and he felt a pang of jealousy that was quickly replaced by a jolt of desire. Sherry had indicated that she wanted more time with Serena but he had no intention of letting her have complete control.

Going to the bed, he gently pushed Sherry aside, then motioned for Serena to come to him. Getting on her knees, Serena crawled to him where he stood stroking his rigid length. She didn't touch him, but wrapped her mouth around him as he guided himself into her mouth. She sucked him hard, taking him in until she almost choked. He tasted so good, so intoxicating and arousing. Her pussy quaked and she felt her thighs shaking again. Then her butt cheeks were spread, a hot tongue slipped between them, moving down until her pussy was once again being licked.

Serena backed up against the thrusting tongue, moaning deeply around James's hard dick. He held the back of her head as he fucked her mouth in long, quick strokes. Sherry fingered her anus and sucked on her clit. Serena was in erotic heaven and just when she thought it couldn't get any better James pulled out of her mouth and turned her to lay on her back, her legs propped up on his shoulders. He sank into her with blissful slowness, watching her as she took all of him into her slick pussy.

"I love you," he mouthed the words and she felt as if her heart would explode with joy. He continued pumping into her and she wondered where Sherry had gone.

Not far because in the next moment the woman's tongue was in her mouth kissing her ferociously as she pinched her nipples.

Serena's climax surpassed any she'd ever had in her life. James carried her to the bathroom and switched on the shower. On shaky legs she stepped inside and let the warm water cascade over her body.

When he was about to close the shower door and leave she reached for him. "No. Please stay with me."

"Are you well rested now?" Nola asked when Mark slipped into her room well after 2:00 in the morning.

"Sorry, I had a few errands to run," he said absently.

"Errands?" Nola sat up and switched on the lamp. "Have you been to St. Michael's before? Do you know people here?"

Mark hesitated, then moved toward her and grabbed her breast. "What's the matter, Nola? You need me to hit you off?"

She pushed his hand away. "I don't need you for anything. I can certainly get myself off! The issue is that you are supposed to be here as my date. You can't do that if you're not around."

He shrugged. "Sorry, it won't happen again."

Nola was fuming. She'd been waiting for him for hours and all he could say was sorry. "Sorry won't cut it," she said and pushed him back on the bed.

His lips spread into a grin. "Are you going to punish me?"

"You bet your arrogant ass I am."

Steven watched her dress, his eyes never swaying from the movement of her hands as she adjusted her bra and slipped into her jeans. His mouth watered and his dick hardened as he noted the way the denim melded to her bottom, fitting firmly between her legs. She pulled a T-shirt over her head and her breasts threatened to bust right out of the material. She clasped the straps to her three-inch sandals then stood in the mirror and adjusted her braids.

Had he ever seen a woman more beautiful?

The answer to that question was what had him speaking before he'd given his words, or her reaction to them, any thought. "I want you to move in with me."

Cally could see him through the mirror. She'd known he'd been watching her and was strangely aroused by that knowledge. But when he spoke, her hands stilled in her hair. "What?"

"When we get home tomorrow night I want you to pack your bags and come and stay with me."

Cally turned slowly, the hairpins she was holding falling to the floor. "Steven, I thought we had an understanding."

"I'm changing the rules."

She shook her head. "You can't."

It was only 8:00 AM so he was still in bed. They'd spent the night making love, because they'd surpassed having sex two days ago, or at least he had. He got out of bed and went to stand in front of her, taking both her hands in his. "I care about you, Cally. I want the opportunity to show you that relationships can work."

"And I need to move in with you for that?"

"If you stay at your place you'll convince yourself that what's between us is the same as what you've had with every other man in your life. You won't give us a chance otherwise."

"No." She tried to pull her hands away but he held firm. "I can't live with you."

"You can, you just don't want to."

She tried to speak but he silenced her with a kiss.

"Think about it while you're out today. Think about you and me."

"This is not what I want," she whispered and touched her lips to his again.

He cupped the back of her head. "Are you sure?" His lips took hers on a sensual journey. A trip down a road of possibilities. With each stroke of his tongue he sought to convince her of what could be and how wonderful it would feel when she got there.

She kissed him in return although her mind screamed that she should run and run fast. Her body felt she was in the right place, enfolded carefully in his arms. Her heart pled for her patience and understanding, it wanted desperately for her to give him a chance, to give them a chance.

The knock on the door told her she needed to hurry up or she'd be late meeting with her mother. And for that they would all surely pay.

Reluctantly, she pulled away from Steven. "I have to go."

He touched her cheek, stroked a finger over her bottom lip. "Think about me today. Not about your past or what you believe your future should be. Just think about me and about us."

Cally nodded and left without another word.

Brunch was at the Old Magic Inn, a place where the Evans family often dined. This morning the table nearest the window with the great view of the river leading out to the Chesapeake Bay was filled with eight women, the sisters and their daughters.

"Why didn't the rest of the bridal party join us?" Nola asked, looking directly at Jenna, who looked spaced-out.

"We thought it would be better if it were just family for a few hours," Marsha stated.

Inside Cally groaned. That meant they were bound to start trippin' about marriage and family again. That was the last thing she was in the mood for this morning. Steven had changed the rules of the game. She wasn't sure why or when but things between them had definitely gone wrong. She couldn't understand. She'd approached Steven the same way she approached everything in her life, with a goal and a purpose. There were parameters that they weren't supposed to cross and she hadn't crossed them. Or had she?

If she really pushed herself she could pinpoint the exact moment when things shifted for her. Yesterday morning, after breakfast, in his car. Sex in the backset of a car parked in a parking garage sounded cheesy and juvenile. There couldn't possibly be any real emotion to the raw act of getting laid out in the open that way. Yet there had been, at least for her. It hadn't been the primal act designed to lead to mutual pleasure. No, this time it had been so much more.

Steven had touched a part of her, a part she wasn't sure even existed. He fed her soul in a way that no man had ever done before. And what truly amazed her was how simply he did it, how it seemed so effortless on his part. He didn't overwhelm her with romance and promises of love forever. What he did was give her facts, then sat back and let her deal with them.

As he'd talked to her yesterday in her uncle's dining room, he flat-out told her that she had no real reason for fearing relationships. She'd thought about that throughout dinner but wasn't ready then to admit that he was right. And when they'd retired to their room that night she'd assumed he would pick up the conversation again; she was actually looking forward to it. But he hadn't said a word.

Instead, he'd touched her ever so gently, removing every stitch of her clothing until she lay naked on the bed. Then he proceeded to worship her body. Not only with his hands and his mouth but with his eyes and his mind. With Steven she visited a place she'd never been before, a place of content. An experience for her to remember for the rest of her life. He didn't say a word last night about them moving in together or his thoughts of this happening. They hadn't spoken a lot except to express satisfaction.

Even that was different. It wasn't so much of the "baby, you feel so good," "fuck me harder" type of expression as it was a melding of minds, a sensed touch, a shared burst of sensation that led to a kiss that communicated far better than words ever could.

She'd known the moment she awakened this morning that things between them were different. But as usual, she'd planned to ignore it and stick to the game plan. Apparently, Steven had a different plan.

"We want to know what's going on," Lorraine said before sipping her coffee.

"What do you mean? We're here because of the wedding," Serena said with confusion. This was definitely not where she wanted to be this morning. Despite her earlier reservations she wanted to be with James. Last night had been revealing to her and she needed time to explore what that would mean for their future. Yes, this morning she'd been considering a future with James Baker again. It was foolish and at least two women at this table would confirm this. But that didn't stop the sweet tingle of possibility inside.

"A wedding. A joyous occasion that should be celebrated with family and friends," Evelyn said. "But we're sensing something else is going on."

Cally looked at Serena, who shrugged and looked at

Nola. All three of them looked at Jenna, whose head was down as she toyed with the food on her plate.

"Jenna?" Leola prodded her daughter gently. "Is there something going on, honey?"

Jenna looked up from her food to find every woman at the table with their eyes on her. "What? What are you talking about?"

"We're talking about the last week in which you've been distant and downright sad when you should be happy and excited about this new life you're about to begin." Marsha sliced her French toast into tiny pieces, speaking as if she weren't discussing anything more meaningful than the weather.

Lorraine nodded and sampled her grits, then added a little more sugar before saying, "And how three women who've adamantly refused to date seriously for the last ten years all of a sudden arrive with men on their arms."

On the opposite side of the table from the older women, the younger women all frowned.

Serena spoke up first, trying to get her defense out of the way. "James just returned to town and I thought it would be nice if he came to the wedding to see everyone."

"You didn't think it would be nice to pick up where you left off?" Lorraine asked her daughter.

"No," Serena spoke truthfully. She hadn't thought about rekindling their prior relationship when she'd first talked to him this week. That silly notion only surfaced in the last day or two. "I just wanted to bring him home to visit the family."

Lorraine nodded but didn't look impressed by her daughter's words.

"I had a chance to meet your young man this morning, Nola. He's a slick one, isn't he? Not quite what I'd expect from you," Evelyn addressed her daughter.

Cally and Serena both remained quiet but they'd thought the same thing when they'd run into Mark this morning. He'd been getting out of his car when they'd walked out onto the porch and introduced himself the moment they saw him. He was handsome and they could certainly see the sex appeal, but there was something peculiar about him that they were sure didn't fit well with Nola.

Nola, who hadn't stopped eating her breakfast during the entire conversation, finished chewing her waffle before speaking. "Don't make too much out of it, Mama. He's a means to an end. I didn't want to show up here alone so I brought him with me. There are no hidden sparks in that department," she said, tossing Serena a grueling look.

"He seemed nice to me," Cally offered and knew instantly that she should have kept her mouth shut.

It was Marsha's turn to address her concerns. "Your man seems to be nice. A doctor is a good catch but I'm afraid he may be a bit out of your league."

Cally choked on her eggs. "Out of my league? What are you talking about?"

"Calathia Margarie Thomas, you know very well what I'm talking about. You have no idea what to do with a man, that's why you haven't had one for so long. While your father and I constantly pray that someone suitable will come into your life since you've hit thirty, we've had our doubts. And now you appear with this man. It's a mixed match, I tell you."

Cally dropped her fork and wiped her mouth briskly with her napkin. "I can date a good guy, Mama. Why is that so hard to believe? And how can you say that some man is out of my league? I'm an independent professional, just like he is."

Serena dropped her head into her hands. She couldn't

believe how this weekend was turning out. It had been her idea—which she'd thought was a good one—to have the men as buffers. Instead, all they did was rouse more questions, making this visit home even more irritating than it had been in the past.

Nola touched Cally's arm in consolation. "I think Steven is a nice guy and if Cally wanted to explore things with him I think she could handle it. However, we all wouldn't feel so compelled to hook up with unsuitable men, even for a weekend, if you three weren't constantly on our backs about marriage."

Lorraine, Marsha, and Evelyn shared a glance, then the eldest of the sisters, Lorrriane, spoke. "We want what's best for you girls, that's all."

"But how do you know what's best for us?" Serena asked. "Mama, you and Daddy have been married for thirty-four years and that's fine for you because you love each other dearly. And Aunt Marsha, you had the love of your life until he passed away. That was tragic, but you learned to live again. Aunt Evelyn, I know that it was hard for you when Nola's father left but you chose to remain alone afterwards. Aunt Leola, you've got a husband who treats you the way you want to be treated. Each of you made a choice in your lives and we wish you'd just let us do the same."

Cally nodded, agreeing with Serena wholeheartedly. Nola even smiled, patting Serena on the hand.

It was Jenna who stole the scene when she attempted to take another drink of her coffee but instead dropped the cup, spilling the hot liquid all over the table. Her hands shook uncontrollably as Aunt Leola instantly rushed to her side. Cally and Serena tried to clean up the mess while the other sisters looked at Jenna and Leola with curious glances.

"Stop babying her, Leola. That's what's wrong with her now. She's spoiled and doesn't know how to stand up for herself," Marsha said.

"Your daughter is no saint, Marsha," Leola tossed over her shoulder.

Marsha chuckled. "That she's not, but at least she has the nerve to stand up to me when she needs to." Looking over at Cally, Marsha couldn't help but smile.

"Jenna knows she can tell me anything," Leola continued. "Right, Jenna? You do know that if there's something bothering you, you can tell me."

Jenna only shook her head. "I don't feel very well."

Because Cally knew her situation, she immediately stood. "Let's go into the bathroom to freshen up," she said to Jenna.

Aunt Leola looked at her strangely but moved back when Jenna stood and turned to go with Cally. With a look, Cally summoned Serena and Nola to join her.

Minutes later Jenna came out of the stall and went to the sink. Her hands shook as she washed them. Any moment now one of her cousins was going to ask her what was going on. And what was she going to say? That she'd had sex with her ex-boyfriend in the bathroom of her uncle's house two nights before her wedding. Or maybe she should try that she was pregnant by her ex-boyfriend and about to marry a man old enough to be her father who she didn't love any more than the valet who'd parked their car.

"All right, what's going on? And don't tell me it's the pregnancy. Something's been bugging you all week long and it's time you spilled it."

Cally sighed. Leave it to Nola to get right to the point. "I think what she's trying to say is it's obvious that something is really bothering you. We can help if you just tell us what's going on."

Jenna moved in what felt like slow motion, wiping her hands on the hard brown towels, then dabbing at her eyes. Looking in the mirror, she saw that she looked a fright. She hadn't gotten much sleep last night and then her mother had awakened her early this morning. She was exhausted and confused and in love with the wrong man.

"I told you I'm pregnant." She took a deep breath and tossed the towels into the trash can. "But it's not Edward's baby."

Serena gasped. "You were cheating on Edward?"

"I knew you were getting yourself some real dick from somewhere. There's no way that old-ass man could be satisfying you." Nola gave her a knowing look.

Cally immediately went to Jenna's side, wrapping an arm around her shoulders. "So what are you going to do? I mean, you can't marry Edward while you're carrying another man's baby."

Jenna shrugged. "I could. He would never guess or if he did he'd make sure nobody else ever found out. Edward needs this marriage. A young wife makes him look hip and has prompted him to make some changes that the board is excited about. This marriage will be a profitable business move for him."

"A profitable business move?" Serena questioned. "Is that the type of marriage you want? What about a loving relationship? A happy home?"

Cally and Nola looked at Serena, but ignored her outburst.

"Marriage is not all it's cracked up to be. You three taught me that. I should have listened. But everybody seemed so happy about Edward and me." Jenna sighed.

"Anyway, I started seeing this other guy about six months ago. It was hot and heavy. The best sex I've ever had."

Nola rolled her eyes impatiently. "What do you know about sex, you're only twenty-five years old? You haven't even reached your peak yet."

"I knew a lot by the time I was twenty-five," Cally said offhandedly.

"I'm sure you did." Nola frowned. "But you weren't sheltered and put on a pedestal like she was. Jenna, I think you're just confused. Our family is very big on marriage and family so they promote it on a regular basis. It's natural that you would feel compelled to follow in your mother's footsteps and marry the first man that asked you. But you don't have to marry him if you don't want to."

"What about the baby's father? Does he know?" Serena asked.

Jenna shook her head. "No."

Cally continued to rub her shoulder. "Are you ever planning on telling him?"

"I don't know what I'm going to do."

"What do you want to do?" Nola asked. "Because in the end that's all that matters. You can't go through life doing things to please everybody else."

"And you can't marry a man you don't love," Cally chimed in. "Marriage should be sacred and it should be based on real feelings and a mutual commitment. It's not to be taken lightly, Jenna. You have to think about this carefully."

"Yeah, maybe you should call it off," Serena suggested. "Talk to the baby's father and then figure out where to go from there. Maybe you and the father could get married."

"Oh please, where are you two coming up with this fairy-tale stuff," Nola huffed. "She can have a baby by herself. It's done all the time. You act like she needs to choose between these men. It's not the end of the world if she doesn't want either one of them."

"It is when I want both of them," Jenna said quietly.

"What?" the three cousins said in unison.

"I'm not like you, Cally. I'm not sure of myself professionally and inclined to believe that having affairs will sustain me for the rest of my life. And I'm certainly not like you, Serena, able to love only one man for my entire life while sleeping with multiple others." Jenna moved away and looked at all three of her cousins standing side by side. "I've looked up to you three for so long. I've wanted to be brash and rigid like Nola and a go-getter like Cally. I've wanted to live your lives as much as I've wanted to escape my own. But then I thought when life gives you peanuts," she said, shrugging, "you've got to make peanut butter."

Serena chuckled. "Granny Elouise used to say that."

"Why can't I have it all?" Jenna proclaimed. "I didn't want children this early, but I can deal with it. I want to marry Edward because he's rich and he's stable and I won't ever want for a thing in my life. And sex with Drew is good, why shouldn't I have that too?"

"Because it's not right, Jenna," Cally said slowly. "If you love Edward enough to marry him you should love him enough to be totally committed to him."

"I didn't say I loved him."

"Then why marry him?" Serena asked.

Jenna sighed wearily. "I told you it's a business deal."

"It's a crock of bull and even I can see that," Nola surmised. "Look, I'm no champion for marriage as it seems some people have become." She tossed Cally and Serena a glance that said she'd deal with them later. "But I'm not an advocate for blatant deceit, either. You need to make a choice. It's not fair to either of these men and, more importantly, it's not fair to this child."

"I know what I'm doing." Jenna moved toward the door. "I'm going to marry Edward and I'll deal with Drew in time. Everything will work out just fine," she said before leaving the bathroom.

Cally groaned and rested her hip against the sink. "Wow. Who would have ever guessed that sweet little Jenna could be such a vixen?"

"I feel so sorry for Edward. I think he genuinely cares for her." Serena shook her head and stepped into one of the stalls.

"Like I said, I'm not for marriage but I despise game-playing. She's going to get burned if she's not careful," Nola proclaimed.

CHAPTER ELEVEN

The rehearsal went as smoothly as one could expect for a bridal party as large as Jenna's. For two hours more than fifty people moved about the sanctuary at the St. Michael's Baptist Church and now were retiring to Uncle's Jeorge's house for the rehearsal dinner.

Cally groaned when she saw the buffet spread of food. Her stomach had been growling for the last hour but she knew that overindulging would have its consequences. She'd be in the gym for hours each day for the next three weeks if she let herself go.

Beside her Steven smiled and talked with members of her family. He hadn't mentioned what they'd discussed this morning before she'd left. When he'd met her at the church he'd kissed her as if they hadn't seen each other in ages. "I missed you," he'd said and she'd confessed to missing him as well.

What did that mean? Could she really miss a man after only a couple of hours, when she'd only been seeing this man for a week? Admittedly what she felt for Steven was unlike anything she'd ever felt before, but Cally was hard-pressed to call it love. Overwhelming lust, maybe. A growing affection would surpass, but love, she still didn't believe she was capable of such a powerful emotion.

And as for moving in with him, well, she hadn't figured that one out yet, either.

Across the room she watched Serena with James. They were hugged up and giggling just like they'd been in high school. It was apparent to anyone who'd known them then that they were in love. And Cally wondered now if they would finally end up together. James said he wanted her back but Serena wanted revenge. Cally got the impression that her cousin's plans were shifting.

Nola, on the other hand, had flirted with one of the groomsmen, a sight that Cally had not seen in a while. Nola usually acted as if a man was the furthest thing from her mind. But tonight she'd worn a very alluring purple dress and heels that practically begged a man to pull up that dress and fuck her where she stood. She was definitely flaunting her goodies and as her law clerk lover made his way into the crowded dining room, she watched Nola make her way to his side.

They were a strange pair, but the sexual tension between them crackled in the air. This would not be the love affair of the century, of that Cally was sure, but it would be interesting to see the ultimate outcome.

Jenna and Edward hadn't been apart since arriving at the church together. To the unknowing eye you would think they were madly in love. Jenna's disposition had drastically improved since she'd left them standing in the bathroom. Cally assumed she'd simply needed to get some things off her chest. Still, she felt kind of sorry for her young cousin, knowing without a doubt that she was making the biggest mistake of her life.

An hour into the evening's festivities Glenda Rawlings, Jenna's wedding coordinator, stood and announced that the bride and groom would now give their bridal party gifts. Several boxes on a cart were rolled in.

Steven had settled into a chair with Cally comfortably perched on his lap. A few seats away from them Serena and James sat sharing a piece of carrot cake. Nola and her man had disappeared a few moments ago, probably to catch a quickie while everyone else was otherwise occupied.

"Jenna and Edward wish to thank all of you for your love and support in this happy time," Glenda was saying.

It didn't take long for the gifts to be opened and thank-yous and hugs to go around the room. Cally was tired and more than ready to go to bed. Tomorrow was Sunday and it was the wedding day. In twenty-four hours she'd have to decide whether or not to move in with Steven. She needed a good night's sleep for that.

"I'm ready for bed," she said as she stood and looked down at him.

"Is that an invitation?" Steven stood, also taking her hand in his.

She smiled, feeling comforted just by the fact that he was there with her. This weekend would have been hard to deal with had she not known that he was there waiting for her. "If you want it to be."

He leaned forward and brushed a soft kiss on her lips. "I always love invitations from you, Cally."

His voice poured over her, as usual, in waves of sensual vibrations. But tonight they sparked something more than just a sexual need. She gladly took his hands and was about to walk out of the room when Glenda spoke again.

"We have one final gift. It arrived this morning for the bride and groom," she chimed happily.

Another rolling cart was pushed in, this one with a television and a DVD player on it. Cally hadn't noticed that Serena and James had come to stand beside her and Steven.

"Will this party never end?" Serena said.

James laughed. "Just wait until it's your turn."

Both Cally and Serena stared at him but didn't have a chance to speak before the television was turned on and the DVD Glenda held was slipped into the machine.

James's remark was the last thing on their minds as they stared at the screen. It was a hotel room or maybe a person's bedroom. There was a huge bed that reminded Cally of the one upstairs in her room.

Then a man appeared. Actually, his toned calves and muscled thighs appeared from behind first. Then tight buttocks and a strong back crossed the screen. There were audible gasps throughout the room but nobody moved to turn the television off.

The man turned to the side, displaying a rock-hard dick jutting forward and ready to poke whatever crossed its path.

Cally swallowed hard.

Serena shifted as James's hand went around her waist.

The man turned, filling the screen with a frontal view of his magnificent hard-on. Hands on his hips, he gave a chuckle then turned his back and whispered something inaudible. In the next instant a woman crawled on the floor toward him. The room was dark so her face was a shadow but her actions were clear. The woman's mouth opened as if she were waiting to be fed. The man didn't move but motioned for her to come closer. She did and he slid his rigid length deep into her mouth.

A few women in the room screamed and ran out. Men hid moans and guffaws. But most stood, transfixed by what they were seeing.

Across the room, Cally spied her mother fanning herself while Aunt Lorraine kept her gaze focused on the screen. Aunt Leola's mouth gaped and both Evelyn and Uncle Jeorge tried to look away.

Neither Cally nor Serena were offended, since they indulged in this sort of entertainment on a monthly basis. However, they never had men around while they did. Cally's nipples tightened and she licked her lips when her attention returned to the screen. The man pumped into the woman's mouth, his length shining with her saliva as he pulled out and pushed back in. Steven's hand went to her ass and squeezed.

The woman clasped the man's tight ass, squeezing as she sucked him hard. Her finger slipped between his crack and fingered his anus. James moved Serena to stand in front of him, pulling her back against his now rigid erection.

Without warning, the man pulled out of the woman's mouth. The woman groaned in protest but he silenced her by putting a finger into her mouth and allowing her to suck once more. Then he lifted her from the floor and took her to the bed. He bent her over until her palms rested on the mattress and with a motion much like that of a police officer making an arrest he spread her legs apart.

With a big palm he smacked her left butt cheek. The woman screeched. He smacked the right cheek and she panted. He grabbed both cheeks and spread them apart then licked her from the top of her crack to her wet pussy.

The room had grown eerily quiet but nobody could vouch for what anyone else was doing because all eyes were riveted to the screen.

The man stopped licking the woman's pussy and stood behind her; stroking his long shaft, he aimed and thrust into the woman with such force she screamed out his name.

"Drew!"

Both Cally and Serena looked at each other in shock.

A second later Nola and Mark came to stand beside them.

"What's going on?" Nola asked. "We were out front and all of a sudden it got quiet in here."

James pointed toward the television and Nola gaped.

The scene had changed. It was another bedroom. The same naked and aroused man but this time the woman was on top of him. Her back was to him as she slid down onto his dick and began to ride. Her breasts bobbed as she moved up and down. The sound of the couple's moaning echoing throughout the room. Again, the faces weren't shown but Nola said slowly, "Oh . . . my . . . God."

Serena and Cally looked at Nola then back to the television.

The man on the screen suddenly sat up, grasping the woman's breasts roughly in his palms.

"Say my name," he growled in the woman's ear.

The woman moaned and continued to ride him.

"Say it!" the man demanded.

The camera shifted and zoomed into the woman's face, starting at her chin and her mouth where she was biting her lip.

"Say it or I'll take this dick from you!"

"No! Don't stop!" the woman crooned. "Please don't stop, Mark!"

In the next instant the woman's face, was revealed and Nola stumbled.

Cally and Serena instantly caught her against them as the room filled with gasps.

On the television several scenes appeared in small boxes around the screen. One was in Nola's office with Nola on her desk, her legs spread wide, Mark licking her pussy freely. Another was of a man, the same man, pumping fiercely into a woman as he held her against the wall. This time the woman was Jenna.

And still another scene showed Mark or Drew or whatever his name was with his legs spread, Nola sucking his dick until his come spurted a couple of feet into the air. The final scene appeared with the man and Jenna in the sixty-nine position on a carpeted floor in front of a fire.

Instinctively, Cally, Serena, and Nola turned to look at Mark, who of course was now gone. Both Steven and James stared at the screen in shock before realizing that Nola was about to pass out beside them.

"What the hell is going on here?" Edward finally yelled.

Jenna sat beside him, calmly rubbing a finger over her bottom lip. Aunt Leola had long since run out of the room with her sisters following her.

The dining room became abuzz with activity and musings. Cally and Serena motioned for the guys to help get Nola out of the room.

"What the hell was that? Did you plan this to stop her wedding?" Cally yelled at Nola when they were on the back porch.

"Don't be stupid," Nola said, raking her fingers through her hair. "I'm just as shocked by that little display as you were." Where was the camera? She'd had no idea that this entire time they'd been together that Mark had been taping her. Or using her, for that matter.

"I can't believe he did this. He gets Jenna pregnant then pursues and tapes you. And where is he now?" Serena looked around. She remembered Mark entering the room just before the second scene of the DVD played. But the moment Nola's face became clear he'd disappeared. She wondered if that had all been a part of his plan.

"Wait a minute, Jenna's not pregnant by her fiancé?" Steven asked.

"Did you know about his affair with Jenna?" Cally asked Nola.

"How could I know, Cally? He works with me, remember. His name is Mark Riley. I got a copy of his personnel file after that morning in my office just to make sure he didn't have a wife and kids at home. I guess employment applications don't ask if you have an ex-girlfriend who happens to be my cousin." She covered her face then let her hands fall to her side, clenching into fists. "Dammit! His name is Mark Andrew Riley. Fuck. He's been pursuing me for about three months now. How long ago did Jenna say she broke up with him?"

Serena thought for a moment. "She didn't."

"Ah, can somebody clue us in to what's going on?" James and Steven stood side by side, staring at the women.

"It seems that Jenna had an affair with a guy named Drew who she's now pregnant by. Drew, who we now know is Mark Andrew, probably decided to get back at Jenna for breaking up with him and slept with Nola," Cally surmised.

"That bastard used me!" Nola screeched.

"It looked like you were having a pretty good time," Serena said, snickering, then covered her mouth.

Cally couldn't help but giggle too. "It did look like you were feelin' it."

Nola rolled her eyes. "Sex is sex. I keep trying to tell you two that. I wasn't in love with him and didn't need to be to get my thing off."

"And you did that quite well," Serena added.

"Shut up." Nola was fuming. She'd sworn all these years that staying away from men would keep her from being hurt or used. But it happened anyway. She felt like strangling Mark Andrew Riley, then thought better of it. She was a better woman than that. Her revenge would be sweet but it would not be misconstrued as a jealous rage, of that she was sure. "He was just a date for the weekend, that's all. But he crossed the line. I don't take kindly to be used."

"You shouldn't take kindly to sleeping with other women's men," Jenna said in a curt tone from the patio door.

The group of five turned to face her.

"How could you?" she said, moving closer to Nola.

"How could I?" Nola asked, confused. "How could he, the lecherous dog. To think that he fucked you last night then came to my room and fucked me. I swear I could kill him!"

"You've always had to have everything. Why couldn't you keep your hands to yourself? I can't believe you would stoop so low as to sleep with my boyfriend!" Jenna raged and before anybody knew what was happening reached out and slapped Nola.

It took Nola a split second to react and then she was lunging for Jenna. Steven grabbed her by the waist and turned her away. "Remember she's pregnant, Nola."

"I don't give a shit. She started it and I'm going to finish it!"

"What is going on out here?" Aunt Leola came out onto the porch, tears streaming down her face, tissues clutched in her hand. "Edward just left in a rage. The guests are talking about that . . . that . . . movie. And you're out here fighting. I don't understand, this is supposed to be a joyous time," she whimpered.

Cally massaged her temples while Serena shook her head. It was a pitiful sight.

The next morning Cally awoke to a warm embrace. She lay on her side, cuddled in Steven's arms. Sunlight streamed through the blinds, casting a golden glow on the otherwise dim room. She sighed with the sheer bliss of the moment.

Everything seemed absolutely perfect, for this one second.

"Good morning," Steven whispered in her ear.

"Mmm, mornin'," she sighed and pushed back further into him.

Steven cleared his throat. "I can only take so much, Cally, and you move quite a lot in your sleep."

Cally smiled. "Sorry." Then she flipped over on her back and stared up at him. "I also want to apologize for the fiasco this weekend has turned out to be."

"Nonsense," he said, tweaking her nose. "I haven't had this much excitement in my life since I was in medical school."

She chuckled. "I just don't know what's going on with my family. I can't believe Jenna's angry with Nola over a guy who was not only cruel enough to sleep with two cousins but to tape it and then show it the night before she was to get married."

"Nola seems more upset with Mark."

"That's a good thing, because if she were focusing her anger on Jenna, you, James, nor my uncles could hold her back." Cally let her arm fall over her forehead. "I just can't believe this is happening. Jenna was supposed to be getting married today. She was supposed to be in love with Edward. This is why—"

Steven covered her mouth and shook his head. "No. That is not why you gave up on relationships. Don't even let that be an excuse."

Cally could only stare at him.

"You're right, Jenna was supposed to love Edward. That's the only reason you should ever agree to marry someone. Obviously, she didn't. If she wanted Mark or Drew or whatever his real name is, she shouldn't have stayed with Edward. That's a personal choice, Cally, it's not the rule."

"I know that her situation was her choice. But you know what, relationships end and people do get hurt. That's not a rule, it's a fact." She tried to sit up but his hands came around her waist, holding her still.

"And life goes on. You can't protect yourself from every bad thing, Cally. And you certainly can't predict what will happen if you try to live a little."

"Did you see the look on Edward's face? I don't want to feel that pain." She took a deep breath. "No, Jenna didn't love him but she was willing to sacrifice that fact for the life that Edward could give her. I don't know if she loved Drew, god, I hope not. But it doesn't even matter, now she's alone and she's pregnant."

"And she knew the consequences of her actions." Steven sat up and pulled her close. "Don't let this stop you from taking a chance on us." He kissed her ear, her neck. "Cally, I want us to be together so badly. I just need you to trust me, to trust yourself to make the right decision."

Cally leaned into his embrace, more confused today than she'd ever been in her life. "There's no way to know for sure if this thing between us will work or not."

"Just like there's no way for you to know that you'll get out of bed tomorrow morning or that you'll make it to bed tonight. It can't be predicted but that doesn't mean we shouldn't try."

Cally closed her eyes, trying desperately to sense what she should do. If her mind wasn't working correctly then she'd rely on her emotions. All she felt right now was the sadness of what Jenna had lost and the fear of what she could have.

But did she really want it? Did she want to be in a relationship, loving and depending on a man that could walk out of her life at any moment?

"No," he whispered, knowing instinctively what she was thinking. "I won't promise you that we'll last forever. But I will promise that I'll do everything in my power to make you happy for as long as I can."

And she believed him. Cally didn't trust men easily and she sure didn't believe whatever lines they tended to spew. But she believed Steven's words because she believed in the type of man he was. He was kind and compassionate and strong enough to push her back when she tried to push him away. She'd thought before that he was the type of man that would stick and now she realized that he was the type that she wanted in her life. So taking the next step seemed inevitable. Steven didn't seem like the type to just want to shack up with a woman, so his request that she move in with him was a little disconcerting. Cally started to analyze that but thought better. If moving in showed Steven that she was serious about him, then she was willing to try it.

She turned to face him, wrapping her arms around his neck. "I don't want promises, Steven." He looked as if he was going to say something so she stopped him with a kiss. "I just want you."

*   *   *

"Somebody really should get married today, Rena," James said as he looked up at her from his position on bended knee.

"You have got to be kidding," was Serena's response.

James chuckled. "No, baby girl, I'm not kidding. I should have asked you this eight years ago before I left. I should have taken you with me. But I can't go back and re-create the past so I'm trying to make the best of our future."

Serena covered her face, afraid to acknowledge his words or the truth she'd see in his face if she did. "No. You're not doing this now. You're not."

Gently, James removed her hands. "Yes. I am." He kissed each palm then looked at her again. "I had planned to ask you this evening when we returned to Baltimore but I figured we both could use something else to occupy our minds right now."

"So this is just a diversion?"

"Don't get all upset because it's not like that. I was going to ask you regardless because I love you." He reached up and cupped her face in his palms. "Do you love me, Rena? Did you ever stop loving me?"

Serena closed her eyes. She'd asked herself that question every day for the last eight years. She knew the answer as well as she knew her own name. "That's not the issue, James."

"It's the only issue. If you love me, say you'll marry me."

She stood and crossed the room. "Love isn't enough. Or at least it wasn't before."

"What are you talking about?"

"I'm talking about how much I loved you eight years ago. How I would have given anything for you to ask me to marry you and for us to go away together. That's the issue,

James. I put my heart and soul into you before and you let me down. Why would I do that again?"

James touched her shoulders and she pulled away. He didn't let that deter him. "I've apologized for that and I've told you that I can't change the mistake I made. But you need to let that go, Rena. You're so busy holding on to what I didn't do, you can't see your part in the demise of our relationship."

Serena turned quickly to face him. "The part I played? What part could I have possibly played?"

"You've been so busy acting like the wounded victim that you failed to see a simple solution. Why didn't you offer to come with me? Why didn't you try to stop me from leaving?"

She opened her mouth to speak, then quickly closed it again. Taking a deep breath, she squared her shoulders and looked at him. "Did you want me to beg you to stay with me? To tell you not to pursue your lifelong goals and instead be my boyfriend? I wasn't going to do that because I cared too much about you. I wanted as much happiness for you that you could find."

"You were being a martyr. You took a gamble and you lost. At any time you could have simply said that you loved me too much to let me go. You didn't have a job lined up after college. There was nothing keeping you in Baltimore besides your loyalty to your cousins. Why couldn't you have been that loyal to me?"

His words hurt. The truth in them all but crushed her. She could have offered to go with him, she could have asked him to stay. But she didn't and she thought she was doing the right thing. Just as he probably thought he was doing the right thing in not asking her to choose. She turned away from him again. "Where do we go from here, James?"

He sighed and went to her again. This time when he placed his hands on her shoulders she didn't pull away. "We move forward. We're still as in love today as we were eight years ago. Even if you don't say it I know it's true." He wrapped his arms around her, pulling her back against his chest. "Let's do the right thing this time, Rena. Let's get married."

This time around Serena refused to be a martyr. She refused to be the strong one, holding out for pomp and circumstance. This time she planned to open her mouth and speak up for what she wanted. "Yes, James. I definitely think we should get married."

Mark Andrew Riley had vanished.

After the rehearsal dinner fiasco and a grueling conversation with her mother and aunts Nola had gone to her room. To wait.

He'd left things there. A bag that she went through thoroughly, a wallet, some money, keys. This told her that he hadn't been prepared to leave the house, that he definitely meant to come back. And when he did she was going to be right there waiting for him.

By morning when he hadn't returned she took matters into her own hands. Getting dressed quickly, Nola crept down the steps, out of the house, and climbed into her car.

An hour and a half later she was at his apartment building about to knock when she decided that a surprise entry would go much better.

Jenna awoke with his hard dick poking into her back. Naked and blissfully content, she scooted back further until his length slipped through her crack.

"You want more already?" he asked as her close confines aroused him.

"I just can't get enough of you," she admitted with a sigh.

"And now you don't have to." With one hard thrust he was inside her heat, her walls grabbing him tightly.

She pushed her butt back, offering herself to him completely. He kissed her neck and her shoulders as he long stroked her for about twenty minutes. By that time they were both ready for the real thing.

Drew came up on his knees and pushed her onto her stomach. He spread her legs wide and traced a finger down her spine. She shivered and he smiled. He caressed her bottom then smacked each cheek and watched it jiggle.

"I love you, baby," Jenna admitted, feeling her excitement gushing between her legs.

"I know you do, boo. And I love you. That's why I couldn't let you marry old boy. You belong to me. I can't live without you," Drew said, then slipped a finger into her hole and pulled it out. Sticking it into his mouth, he tasted her. "I will never get enough of tasting you, Jenna. Show me my pussy."

Jenna loved when he talked to her that way. She instantly came up on her knees, reaching her hands around to spread her cheeks so he could get an unfettered view of her offerings.

Drew wrapped his hand around his rock-hard dick and stroked. Her pussy lips glistened with her arousal, her hole opening like a waiting mouth for him to feed. Come oozed from his slit and he wiped it off with his finger and wrote his name on her ass. "You belong to me, Jenna. You know that, don't you?"

Jenna wiggled her bottom, knowing how much he liked that. "Yes, Drew. I belong to you."

He thrust inside of her so hard her head slammed into

the headboard. She screamed but he kept thrusting, pumping mercilessly into her pussy. Jenna gasped as he took her hard from the back. She loved this position because he went so deep she could feel him in her lower stomach. His dick filled her until she felt like she would burst. With all his strength he pumped into her and her body accepted him. She backed her ass up against each thrust, moaning and panting as she did.

How did she ever think she could live without this? It just wasn't possible.

"More. I want more of you. Turn around," Drew commanded.

Jenna turned around and lay flat on her back.

"Hold your legs up."

She did and he lowered his head, licking up and down her labia, taking all her essence into his mouth. He fingered her clit, then sucked on it until she squirmed beneath him. Plunging two fingers into her hole, he continued to suck her pussy until her entire body convulsed and she came in his mouth.

Drew scooped her into his arms and carried her to the dresser, where he knocked the contents to the floor and sat her on the cool surface. Pushing her legs apart, he impaled himself in her to the hilt. Jenna wrapped her legs around his waist, securing their connection. He began to pump, her slickness causing a gushing sound as he did.

Drew worked her pussy until his own legs began to shake. "I'm about to come, baby. How do you want it?"

Her nails sank into the skin of his shoulders and she bit on her bottom lip. "I want it in my ass. You know I like it there, Drew."

Drew pulled out of her quickly and turned her around, pushing her down so that her breasts smashed against the surface. His dick was drenched from her juices. Still he licked his fingers and rubbed them along her anus, slipping the first half of his fingers inside to loosen her up. Jenna wiggled and his dick pulsated, pre-come oozing out of his slit. "Oooh baby, I can't wait another minute."

He pushed the tip in, holding her gyrating hips steady as he did. "Keep still, Jenna, or I'm going to bust right now. Let me get it in first."

Jenna tried to keep her bottom still as he sank inch by delicious inch of his dick into her ass. When he was buried completely, he groaned, then pulled out and sank in again.

"Now, baby. Please, come inside me now!" Jenna begged.

"Mmm, I love it when you beg. I love you so much, boo." Drew pumped twice more then felt his dick pulse and empty its sweet milk deep into her hole.

"Oh, Drew," Jenna sighed.

"Yes, oh, Drew," Nola said from the doorway. "I happen to know from experience that Mark—or excuse me, *Andrew*—is especially good in this position."

Drew turned to face her, his dick slipping slowly out of Jenna. "What are you doing here?" he asked with nothing short of disgust.

Jenna turned. "Nola?"

"Isn't this convenient?" Nola walked closer, her hands buried in the pockets of her jacket. "You expose our affair in front of the entire bridal party and yet you still get the prize." She shook her head. "I thought so much better of you, Jenna."

"Nola, you have no idea what you're talking about. Drew and I have been through a lot. We belong together."

"Then you're just as sick as he is," Nola spat.

Drew moved in front of Jenna, pushing her safely behind him. "What do you want? You made it perfectly clear that this was just a fling. No harm, no foul."

"Except there was some foul. From the moment you walked into my office and put your mouth between my legs, I should have known you were foul. You were fucking me and my cousin at the same time, that's beyond foul." As she spoke Nola pulled her hands out of her pocket and aimed the gun.

"Nola!" Jenna exclaimed.

Drew only frowned. "You don't have the nerve. You're cool and intelligent in the courtroom and you're very interesting in bed, but you are *not* a killer."

Nola smiled. "You're partially right. I'm not a killer," she said, then lowered the gun to his groin and fired. "And I'm beyond interesting in bed. I'm fucking fantastic!"

Nola turned, hearing a screaming Jenna and a howling Drew behind her as she did. She walked calmly out of the room, not bothering to look back.

CHAPTER TWELVE

Three Months Later

"The lawyer got you a really good deal," Cally said from the other side of the raggedy table where she and Serena sat across from Nola.

They were in the state penitentiary, visiting their cousin a week after her plea bargain had been accepted in court. Nola had driven all the way back to St. Michael's after being in Drew's apartment. She'd knocked on both Serena and Cally's bedroom doors and asked them to meet her in the dining room. There, amidst Steven and James, she told them that she'd shot Drew's balls off because it's what he deserved.

An hour later the police were at the door. Aunt Evelyn was hysterical. It took all three of her sisters and her brother to carry her off to her room. Steven drove along with James in the front seat and Cally and Serena holding hands, crying in the backseat, to the police station. Through it all Nola remained her calm, cool, and collected self. She never explained her story beyond the fact that Drew was disgusting and didn't deserve to fuck another woman. Serena joked that Nola had done what millions of women only dreamed of.

"He should have, I paid him enough money," Nola said smartly.

"Are you going to be able to handle it?" Serena asked.

Nola waved a hand. "Six months jail time and three years probation. It'll be fine. I've already got three months in. It's not so bad in here."

"Not so bad?" Cally said, looking around. "I guess it wouldn't be if you're a lesbian."

"Don't be fooled, Cally girl. There's more than enough dick behind bars." Nola smiled.

Later that evening, after their cells were locked and the lights were ordered out, Nola heard familiar footsteps. Her pussy pulsated with each step. She lay on her cot, in her cell alone because her cellmate had asthma and always seemed to get extra time out in the yard during the hot afternoons.

She toyed with her breasts, feeling the stiff nipples between her fingers. The footsteps stopped and she cracked her eyes to see the huge shadow standing on the other side of the bars. Keys clinked and turned in the lock and then the bars slid open. She sat up in the bed.

The bars closed but he was on the inside now. He came closer, his six-foot-eight stature and bulky frame filling the small cell. Nola leaned back on her arms and waited.

"Is that for me?" he said in that deep voice that made her wet.

Nola spread her legs and smiled. "It's all for you, Sergeant Matthews."

His beefy arms lifted her from the mattress and pushed her against the wall. Nola fidgeted with his belt buckle and zipper, knowing they didn't have a lot of time. His huge dick fell into her hands and she licked her lips.

"Not this time, boo. I need to be inside of you. Daddy's been thinking about this all day long," Sgt. Gerard Matthews groaned into her ear. "Put me into that hot pussy you know I love."

Nola did just as he said, placing the fat head of his dick at her entrance, then holding her breath as he slipped inside. Gerard was a big man, all over. The first time he'd come into her cell and demanded she strip for him, Nola had been cocky and sure she could withstand whatever he did to her. But the moment he stuffed his full length inside of her she'd thought he'd rip her in two. But Gerard had been gentle, working her sugary walls until they were accustomed to his size.

His shift was five days on and four days off. For four days she was forced to bring herself to climax with only the memory of his heavy hands on her as a guide. But for those five days on, she could expect him every night an hour after lights-out. Tonight was no different.

"You taking this dick tonight, aren't you baby?" he groaned, pumping into her until her back was flat against the wall.

"Yes," she whimpered because she was taking him and with pleasure.

Another three months in here was going to be just fine with her. She had only begun wondering what would happen with her and Sgt. Matthews when she was released. Nola didn't want a permanent man, but if it meant she was going to be sexed like this on a regular she just might reconsider.